The Archaeologist's Daughter

Under the Shadow of the Marquess
Book One

SUMMER HANFORD

CLAIRMONT
HOUSE

ISBN: 978-0-9980815-7-1
ISBN 0-9980815-7-4

Cover design by dreams2media
Stock Photography HotDamnDesigns

First Trade Paperback Printing February 2018

10 9 8 7 6 5 4 3 2

www.scarsdalepublishing.com

CHAPTER ONE

William Greydrake, future Marquess of Westlock, lounged on the leather couch in Lethbridge's London office, watching the attorney shuffle pages. The room, furnished in dark wood, was perpetually gloomy. It suited its occupant.

"Have you any brandy?" William asked. "If I must endure your paper pushing, I should like a drink."

Lethbridge darted a look at the clock on his mantel. "It's eleven in the morning."

"You're the one who cried urgency. It's inhumane to drag a man from his bed at this hour, and more so not to compensate for it with a snifter."

"I haven't any brandy." Lethbridge's words were clipped. He pulled free a page.

"You ought to. The old man pays you enough."

William could read the frown pinching the attorney's already narrow features. He'd seen the look often enough, on so many faces, to know what Lethbridge saw. A tailcoat creased from being worn all night. An untied cravat. William's disheveled brown hair. His still shiny boots, propped on the furniture.

He was the image of an indolent nobleman's son. Owner of the world. Careless and carefree. It was obvious to anyone who saw William that he'd been out all night, likely gambling, drinking, and enjoying lightskirts. He wore his depravity proudly before the world.

That was how he arranged to appear. His reputation could even explain the occasional black eye. With the marquess's men watching him, he must jealously guard his true nature, his actual dealings. The old bastard had well-ingrained the price of not conforming to his ideas of what a peer should be.

William leaned his head back on the couch. He studied the ceiling until he properly blotted out the repercussions of falling short of the marquess's expectations. He dropped his gaze and traced the dark wood paneling with his eyes, skimming over the small door that closed off Lethbridge's record room.

He adopted an indolent smile and focused on the attorney. "Exactly why am I here?"

"Your father asked me to draw up a list of acceptable brides for you." Lethbridge proffered a page.

"Brides?" Maybe he really did need that drink. "I have four more years of freedom. The marquess is of the opinion no worthy gentleman weds before thirty."

"He has changed his mind." Lethbridge set the page down on the edge of his desk. "He wishes to ensure you marry correctly."

William drummed his fingers. "Why now?"

Lethbridge drew in a breath, his expression more serious than usual, no mean feat. "Lord Westlock is dying."

Feet slamming to the floor, William came upright on the couch. "Don't toy with me, Lethbridge."

"I assure you, I do not."

Giddiness swept through him. "Are you certain? He's sought a doctor's opinion? A priest's? We wouldn't want to be wrong about this." Could the joyous day finally be at hand? William grinned. A world without the marquess was wonderful to contemplate.

"He is certain, as is his physician." Lethbridge's face remained bland, but his eyes went dark with disgust.

"Don't look at me like that, Lethbridge." William stood, restive. "The old man is a bastard and a half and you know it. He all but killed my mother."

Lethbridge dropped his gaze. "Your mother killed his heir, your older brother. She was ill, mentally unfit. The marquess could have seen her hang, but instead he installed her in a facility where she could get the care she needed. I'm sure they did all they could to help her."

"My mother was not a murderer, or mad." William's voice was low as he struggled for an even tone.

"I'm sure you have fond memories of her. You were what, four when she was removed? But I assure you, I've seen the papers. A competent doctor declared her unfit."

"Yes, I know." A doctor the marquess paid off. "She was violent and unfit. The old man was wracked with grief. Too overcome to set eyes on me, he shipped me, a child of four, off to Mr. Darington in Egypt. Common knowledge." And all a lie.

"Exactly. It therefore behooves you not to delight in your father's decline."

"Tell me this, why was I such a terrible reminder? The world knows I am the image of the marquess. Nothing about me speaks of my mother." Every mirror a reminder. "While you're prevaricating, explain as well how the man can have the devil's own luck with wives. One a mad murderess, one fallen to her death, and a third too ill to remain in England?"

"I'm sure I don't know what you're insinuating. The marquess is a great man and worthy of your respect."

William ran a hand across his hazel eyes, in an effort at calm. Lethbridge was the marquess's man through. There was no sense arguing with him. Besides, if the old bastard really was dying, it would soon be moot. His spirit buoyed by the prospect of the marquess's death, William pulled his composure about him.

Eyes open, his attention caught on the page at the edge of the desk. A list of names. A few lines at the bottom. He crossed to scoop it up. "These are the women, then?"

Lethbridge nodded. "He ordered you to sign it, to agree you will marry one."

William crossed to the fireplace. Behind the clock on the mantel hung the dreariest landscape he'd ever encountered. Beneath, the fire wasn't lit. That would make the room too inviting. Coals glowed red in the grate, though. Perhaps when he was alone, Lethbridge permitted himself to be comfortable.

Leaning on the mantel, William studied the page. What a list. Diamonds of the first water, to be sure. Women with ice in their veins, all of them. The sort of women a man could never know happiness with, likely not even pleasure. Diamonds had sharp edges, after all.

His eyes caught on a name near the bottom of the page. Lady Lanora Hadler, the archaeologist's daughter. "You said you drew this up?"

"Your father left it to my discretion, after setting his parameters." Lethbridge sounded proud.

William cast a look over his shoulder, not hiding his disdain. Lethbridge smoothed back his stringy brown hair, used a kerchief to wipe the oil from his hand. Only the attorney would be proud to be asked to draw up such a list. The marquess's toady, hopping at the chance to please.

William reread the name. The marquess would never have included Lady Lanora, only child of Robert Hadler, Duke of Solworth, a man much respected by the Royal Society for his work uncovering the secrets of Egypt. The marquess had no use for learned men, even dukes, but especially avoided

Solworth. If anyone could uncover the secret of William's past and tarnish the Greydrake name, it was the archaeologist.

Interest tugged at William. He'd long wished for words with the duke. In Egypt, Solworth worked in parallel with his fellow archaeologist, Mr. Darington. A man William had never met, despite well-circulated information to the contrary. Darington, who lied for the marquess, yet, somehow, was the only man William trusted.

Not that courting Lady Lanora would bring her father. It was common knowledge the Duke of Solworth hadn't set foot in England in a dozen years. More than that, William had spotted Lady Lanora across many a ballroom. Though she had alluring midnight locks, sculpted features and lush curves, she inspired little desire in him. If women of her caliber had ice in their veins, Lady Lanora's were frozen solid. It was a wonder she could move, let alone with such grace, given how rigid she was. She struck fear into the hearts of most men. Those who dared ask her to dance generally fled after one set.

William studied the coals in the grate, contemplating remembered glimpses of the black-haired beauty. His gaze caught on a scrap of paper in the ash, and he suppressed a start of surprise. The handwriting, so familiar, couldn't be mistaken. Darington's. William knew Darington was a client, referred by the marquess. What could warrant burning?

Surely not the list. Darington wouldn't have anything to do with such high-handedness. Besides, the man wrote so often of his daughter, William had long since realized Darington hoped for the connection. Reading of her kind heart and generous nature, William often did as well, but Darington's daughter wasn't the sort of woman who would make Lethbridge's list. Too low, and far too kind.

William took the page back to the desk and dropped it onto the dark wood. "None of these women will have me."

"Perhaps if you mend your behavior." Lethbridge's tone was tentative.

William snorted. "The marquess requested a life bereft of sentiment or compassion, lived only for pleasure. Now, he wishes me to appeal to these?" He tapped the page.

"Some would agree for your wealth. Some for your title."

"What if I refuse?" William sat on the edge of Lethbridge's desk, carefree demeanor employed with practiced ease. "The old bastard asks much, after all. This isn't like demanding I flaunt my circumstance among the *ton*. This is marriage. Misery for all my days." At least, it would be with any of the women listed. His eyes drifted to the fireplace and the words among the ashes.

Lethbridge frowned, craning his head at an uncomfortable angle to look up at him. "Then the marquess requested I inform you he had me draw up a second will. He hasn't signed it, but he shall, if you do not concede to his demand."

"Oh?" William drawled. "And what does this dreadful second will do that the first did not?"

"Leaves your half-sister everything but the entailed ancestral lands, which will be bankrupted without the rest."

"Madelina? She's sixteen. Who would run the estate?"

"I would."

Did William imagine the avaricious glint in Lethbridge's mud-colored gaze? "You," he repeated, tone flat.

"I will be her guardian until she's of age, or until I give her permission to wed." Lethbridge squared his thin shoulders, snapped the stack of papers nearest him straight and set them back in place.

"So, my choices are to thaw the heart of one of these diamonds, or end up a pauper on a bankrupt estate?" William had plans for the marquess's money. It didn't surprise him the old man had conjured up a final hurtle.

"That is one way to see it, yes."

"It is the only way to see it." William pushed a hand through his hair. "Fine, I'll marry a debutant off your list. How difficult can it be to find one willing to become a marchioness?"

"Excellent." Lethbridge opened a drawer and pulled out a neatly trimmed pen. "You made the right choice." He reached for the inkwell and slid it across the desk to a spot on William's left. He set the pen beside it.

William wondered if Lethbridge was being thorough or intended to needle him by remembering he was left handed. The marquess considered it a defect in character. He'd paid many tutors to break the habit. Only, William's writing instructors had failed. In all other matters, William could appear, as the marquess put it, respectable.

His eyes sought the mantel clock. He wasn't actually one for drinking early, but it was drifting toward midday. Somewhere, outside of Lethbridge's gloom-filled office, there was daylight to walk through, his club, and a bottle waiting. William felt a greater than usual need for a drink.

His gaze drifted to the grate. He tried not to feel the loss of Darington's daughter. She was a dream. He'd never met the girl. Besides, he could always hope the marquess died before he managed to win one of the diamonds. William took up the pen, and signed.

"The marquess has given you a score of days. After that, he will sign the new will." Lethbridge had read William's mind.

William tossed the pen on the desk. He took delight in the ink blot, and how Lethbridge scrambled for his kerchief to wipe it up. "I surely hope that's enough business for today," William said.

Lethbridge didn't look up as he scrubbed at the ink. "There's still the matter of Miss Chastity."

William frowned, on guard. "My mistress? What of her?"

"If you're to marry, will you be keeping her? Another payment for her townhouse is due." Lethbridge's eyes darted toward him, then away.

A test, William thought. The old man put the words in Lethbridge's mouth. William contained a smile. He knew the correct answer. "Gads, man, what sort of question is that? I don't see what marrying has to do with my mistress."

"You don't mean to, that is, love your wife?" Lethbridge grimaced as the words came out.

"I haven't spent the past twelve years learning to be fashionable to ruin it all by falling in love. You can tell the marquess I said as much." Besides which, William took his responsibilities seriously. Chastity would be maintained as she was until the marquess was cold and buried. William would not give her up. No wife would change that.

CHAPTER TWO

Lady Lanora Hadler, daughter of the Duke of Solworth, sat at the kitchen table in her father's London home, shucking peas. Her best friend and maid, Grace, was opposite her, similarly engaged. Lanora's hands flew as she stripped the ripe green pods, but Grace was still winning. Her pile was nearly gone.

"Victory," Grace cried, eyes bright, dropping a final pod onto the heap of shells before her.

Lanora smiled. "I don't know how you do it, or how you can be so nimble with peas and not able to stich a straight seam." She kept working. The peas were needed for dinner.

"Practice." Grace reached across the table and snatched some of Lanora's.

Lanora pushed a dark lock from her eyes. "You could practice sewing."

"But then you'd want me to do it. I prefer kitchen work. Someday, when you wed, you'll set up your own home, and I'll be your cook."

"I will never wed, but you are welcome to cook all you like once I convince Father I need my own home."

"Or that." Some of the cheer left Grace's face.

"I will convince him." Lanora snapped a pod open with such vigor, some of the peas jumped out. "He must acknowledge I'm perfectly well on my own." She made a vague gesture around the kitchen.

It was a warm room, the plaster walls yellow in the morning light. The sunshine that spilled through the windows gave way to a view of the garden, hothouse and grounds beyond. Lanora knew the grounds were large for London, but had never fully taken to them. The ordered patch of earth was worlds away from the rolling hills and forest around her country home.

She sighed, and slowed. She didn't hate London. She simply wished her father hadn't decided she must have a season. She missed the people left behind, though many of the staff had made the journey with her and she'd come to know the London staff well. She missed the countryside, the tenants and freedom. Not freedom from oversight, for she was ordered about no more in London than the countryside, but of space and from the scrutiny of the *ton*.

Lanora's chaperone, her Aunt Edith, was even more opposed to London living than she was. The frumpy middle-aged sister to Lanora's father, Aunt Edith was likely riding in the park even then. Riding or not, she wore mostly riding habits, and those about two decades out of fashion. To make London more tolerable, Aunt Edith had brought many of her terriers to town with her, the little monsters her one true love. Lanora found them enjoyable in the countryside, but they chafed at the small grounds, too little work making them ill mannered.

Still, their London cook said the larder had never been so vermin free. She plead endlessly with Aunt Edith to leave a few of the little mongrels behind. Likewise, the groundskeeper was impressed with the lack of small creatures ravaging his work. For her part, Lanora missed the songbirds. If a pair was foolish enough to remain on the grounds, the terriers would wait for the fledglings to leave the nest and snap them up before they learned to fly properly.

"You're wearing your dead-baby-songbird face," Grace said. She took up the last of Lanora's peapods.

"I do wish new ones wouldn't keep coming."

Grace shrugged. "It's nature." She finished the peas and stood, gathering the shells for the bin. "I was thinking. I should win a prize for shucking more peas than you."

Lanora narrowed her eyes. "Such as?"

"Such as, for today, you forget about Mrs. Smith."

A broad smile turned up Lanora's lips. Mrs. Smith, the only wonderful thing about London. Not that the reason for her was good. Poverty was never a happy circumstance, and poverty was what Mrs. Smith sought to alleviate. Rather, Lanora sought to alleviate it, in the guise of the widowed Mrs. Smith.

Lanora was quite enamored with being unknown enough to wander the streets. At home, her midnight locks and deep green eyes were too easily recognized, even with a cap and spectacles. There were so many people in London, and the wealthy kept themselves so far above the rest, no one Lanora helped as Mrs. Smith had any notion who she really was.

Mrs. Smith was much preferable to her evening role, duke's daughter. Maintaining that frigid façade was an endless strain. Lanora had little choice, though, if she wanted to survive the season unattached and go on to have a home of her own. All she wished was to keep living the unfettered life she'd enjoyed since her father began his work a dozen years ago.

Besides, the smiling faces and pleasant conversation offered by her so-called peers were as much a pretense as her coolness. No one in London knew her, so how could they like her? Their warmth sprang from regard for her father's title, or his wealth, or both. Perhaps even from his notoriety as a scholar, but never from caring for Lanora. She'd learned well enough from her charitable works at home the lengths to which his assets would drive people. For most, Lanora was a chance for money, renown or power, nothing more.

"Now you're wearing your, no-one-loves-me-for-who-I-really-am look." Grace reseated herself.

"You know me too well." Lanora sought her earlier light mood.

"I know you very well. You're like a sister to me, and I assure you there are many people who love you."

"Here, in this house, and in Father's country manor, yes." Lanora waved a hand toward the windows. "Out there? No. They will never come to know me. All they see is Lady Lanora, only child to Lord Robert, Duke of Solworth."

"You give them no chance to know you." Grace's voice took on an imploring note, "If you would, you may find you come to enjoy the company of some of them. Perhaps even a gentleman. You're too young to have decided never to marry."

Lanora let out a sigh. "Not this lecture. Not again."

Grace's mouth flattened in a mutinous line, but she shrugged. "Well then, about Mrs. Smith--"

"I don't have all that bread sent to let it be distributed improperly. You know if Mrs. Smith isn't there to hand out what she paid for, the first people will take more than their share and sell it to those I mean to have it free. The rector of the church is too kind. He's taken in by any story."

"You go too often. Too many of them know the Widow Smith now. What if one sees you elsewhere? Word will get back to the rest. The poor feed on gossip."

Only because they have no real food much of the time. "No one will recognize me."

"That's not my true worry, as well you know." Grace's features tensed. "Walking the streets of London alone is foolish for any woman, but you, a duke's daughter, are in even more danger."

"Again, I assure you, no one will recognize me."

"Black hair is not common, and yours has been mentioned in the paper." Grace looked triumphant, as if that point couldn't be overcome.

"The people I help are hardly literate." Something that should be remedied.

"Even if they are, I doubt they're reading gossip about debutants. They have better uses for their time." Like trying not to let their children starve.

"They may not read about you, but they hear things, and repeat them."

"I powder my hair, tie it up and wear a bonnet when I'm Mrs. Smith." The powder trick had only worked a short while at home, what with country gossip, but in London, Lanora felt it would last.

"I know. I'm the one who has to clean up after it."

"I help," Lanora said, stung.

Grace shook her head. "You're as good at tidying as I am at sewing." She pursed her lips. "I'm serious, Lanora. Gentlewomen get kidnapped in London. If you're lucky, you'd be recognized and ransomed. If not, they'll sell you into a house of ill repute. I've heard the stories."

Lanora laughed. "And stories are all they are. You're being dramatic." Mischief brightened her mood. "Besides, if I'm kidnapped, maybe your Lord Lefthook will come to my rescue."

Grace's expression shifted from worry to a silly, moon-eyed look. She let out a sigh. "If only he really was my Lord Lefthook."

Lanora rolled her eyes. "How you can be so enamored with a man you don't even know is beyond me."

"Don't pretend you aren't there each morning, right beside me, scouring the paper for his name."

"And such a silly name," Lanora said, ignoring that truth. "Lord Lefthook. Couldn't the editor come up with something better?"

"They say it's on account of his tremendous left hook." Grace mimed a punch, eyes wide in an equally round face.

"And the lord part?" Lanora's voice was thick with derision.

"On account of his noble deeds."

Lanora had to admit they did sound noble, if one believed the paper. "They're likely made up. He's likely made up, to sell more copies. Every parlor in London has the paper in it now, right by the tea tray. Ladies send out for their own, not wanting to wait for their male relations to finish with their copies."

"His deeds are not made up." Grace's jaw jutted out. "I have it from the butcher's wife that the baker cross town, on Southway, has a client who was set upon one night past sundown and saved by Lord Lefthook. He's telling true, too. It was in the paper."

"And did the baker relate this tale to the butcher's wife before or after he read it in the paper?"

Grace frowned. "And they had that quote, last week, from that woman Lord Lefthook saved. The one coming home through the park alone."

"I suppose you think that woman is real, as well?" Lanora gave a sad shake of her head. "As if any woman would come home through the park alone, at night. You're the one who's too naive for London, Grace, not me."

"They wouldn't print it if it wasn't true," Grace said with conviction.

"Even if the deeds are real, do you mean to believe there's but one Samaritan in all of London?" Lanora smiled. "He's awfully busy, doing good deeds nearly every night." Lanora loved to tease Grace, but she was interested in the figure of Lord Lefthook. Real or imagined, his work brought needed attention to poor parts of London, for that's where he roamed.

Since arriving, she'd been horrified by the conditions that existed in the city. No one under her father's care was permitted to live in such poverty. She would take the forgotten of London back to the country with her if she could, but there were simply too many. Something must be done where they were, in London, to rectify the problem. Especially for the women and children, many of whom bore no fault for their circumstance.

Reminded of the other reason she especially wished to go out, Lanora stood. "I am going, and that's the last of it."

"I won't help you ready. I disapprove."

Lanora shrugged. "That's your right, of course." She headed upstairs to don her disguise. Grace would follow soon.

Today, once she finished handing out bread, Lanora intended to track down Mr. Finch and have words with him. Mr. Finch was the foreman in charge of building a newly begun home for displaced women, including those with children but no father for them. Last time she spoke with him, he'd assured her that work was about to resume, but it still had not. Lanora was particularly invested in the structure, for she'd begged her father to fund it. Her time in London told her a home for women was the area of greatest need, the way to help the most people.

Her father hadn't put up the money. He'd given some nonsensical excuse about being a peer, and the politics of the land being resistant to change. Instead, to appease her, he talked his fellow archaeologist, Mr. Darington, into funding the project.

Lanora had never met Mr. Darington, something of a mythical figure to the *ton*. Every month came word of daring deeds, exotic queens and foreign dangers. On top of that, precious, rare and beautiful artifacts. He was the reverse of her father, who kept quarters in Cairo, while directing excavations, analyzing finds and writing scholarly works.

Not that her father didn't make excellent contributions to the study of Egypt. He'd located several key sites. It was inevitably Mr. Darington, who'd been working in obscurity for years before her father arrived in Egypt, who excavated them. Her father waited in the relative safety of Cairo for the artifacts to reach him. He was the intelligence behind their years of success, Mr. Darington the dashing figurehead.

One of the reasons Lanora consented to a season was the chance to meet Mr. Darington's protégé, Lord William Greydrake, only son of the Marquess of Westlock. Lord William had spent his formative years living in the desert with Mr. Darington, before her father arrived. Though he was eight years her senior, Lanora had expected to find a kindred spirit in Lord William.

Lanora's mother passed away when she was six. Her father, unable to cope with the loss of his wife, ran off to Egypt. Lanora spent a few years with her grandfather, before he too passed. When Lord William's family suffered their tragedy in his youth, his father sent him to Egypt, to Mr. Darington. Though opposite, Lanora's and Lord William's lives were strangely parallel.

Lanora shook her head as she entered her room. She began undressing, able to do most of it herself. Mrs. Smith wore the same undergarments as Lanora did, since no one would ever see them to know they were too fine for a widow who spent all her extra funds feeding the poor.

She still hadn't met Lord William, and no longer cared to. One look at him across a ballroom had convinced Lanora the years with Mr. Darington hadn't done him any good. Lord William exuded rakishness. Tousled brown hair, flecked with gold by candlelight. A long, lean frame clad somehow both impeccably and carelessly. His crooked smile, always touched with indolence. Glinting hazel eyes that changed color with his mood.

Grace's footsteps sounded in the hall. Lanora shook her head to dispel visions of Lord William and resumed undressing. Handsome though he was, it had taken only one look for her to be sure she had no care for Lord William's hazel eyes, or his moods. On top of his discernable rakishness, his name appeared in the scandal sheets with the consistency of the sunrise. Lanora wasn't in London on the hunt for a husband, or even friends. If she ever did want either, Lord William Greydrake was the last man in England she'd choose.

CHAPTER THREE

William knocked. The townhouse stood on a street outside the most fashionable part of London. The neighborhood was safe, maintained, and known for housing the mistresses of London's most wealthy men. He waited, not begrudging the time it took for Lady Cecilia's maid to open the door. The girl could be anywhere in the house. He would give Cecilia more servants, but that would only increase the chance the marquess would find her.

"My lord," the maid said as the door swung open.

"Is Miss Chastity at home?"

"She's always at home to you, my lord." The girl gave him a knowing smirk.

William offered a look somewhere between amused and bored. The girl backed inside, leaning forward as she curtsied. It would take a better man than William not to avail himself of the view her low neckline offered, but he was eager to see the lady of the house. He brushed past the maid and jogged up the steps to Cecilia's private chambers. Once there, he looked up and down the hall and knocked softly. It was a courtesy no man would pay his mistress.

"Enter," she called.

William entered to find his stepmother, Lady Cecilia Greydrake, third wife to the marquess, seated near the window. She stood, and smiled. He closed the door and offered a bow.

"You're early," Cecilia said.

"Please, sit." William crossed the thick carpet to take the chair opposite hers as she sat. "I have news."

"Good news?" she asked brightly.

Four years his junior, Cecilia had an effervescent quality that matched her spritely features and build. William could only thank God he'd removed her from the marquess before that joy was beaten out of her. She smiled at him now, her look expectant.

When William's first stepmother, his sister Madelina's mother, had mysteriously fallen to her death after her forth miscarriage, William had hoped the marquess wouldn't remarry. He'd done all in his power to appear the perfect son, to give the old man no reason to want a third wife. Apparently, his powers were limited. In William's twentieth year, the marquess brought a sixteen-year-old Cecilia into their home, and the nightmare began again. William had been too young to save Madelina's mother or his own, but, so far, he hadn't failed Cecilia.

He stretched out his legs. A smile crept over his face, despite his dark thoughts. "The marquess is dying."

Cecilia's mouth dropped open. She shut it. "Are you certain?"

He nodded. "Lethbridge is."

She leaned forward, eager. "Is he very ill?"

"We can only hope so. I haven't been to see him, but I will."

Her expression shifted to concern. "You don't need to. Not on my account. I've waited six years. A bit more won't hurt."

"I want to see him for myself." William grimaced. "Maybe I can get out of the new torment he's devised for me."

"You mean, beyond demanding you conduct yourself as the most pompous, destructively wealthy rake in London?"

He grinned. "That was never his exact order. He said I must prove I'm not soft like my mother. No caring for anyone beneath me, no charity, no compassion. I added in the rake business." He affected a bored tone. "He left me few avenues for happiness."

Cecilia wrinkled her nose. "Ply your act somewhere else, William. I know you aren't a rake. You use those clubs and private rooms just as you do this house, as cover."

He shrugged. He did. Sometimes, it grew difficult to give up the act, even with Cecilia. He'd played a bounder for over a decade. "I won't need to for much longer."

She gave him a happy smile. "And I won't need to hide in this house. Do you know how long it's been since I stepped outside these walls?" She turned her face toward the window, leaning into the streaks of orange light from the setting sun.

William clamped his mouth shut over a reprimand. He didn't like her to get too close to the windows. Even after so many years, the marquess routinely set men to follow him. Though William never provided any evidence, the old man seemed to sense his son wasn't who he wished. William unclenched his hands from the arms of the chair. Cecilia's rooms were on the back side of the house. He was being overcautious.

Or was he? She had only a week in the marquess's clutches to go by. His mother survived seven years before fleeing with William. After they disappeared, the marquess had her declared a murderess, mad, and then dead. Later, when he had William back, he invented the fiction of Egypt to cover William's decade-long disappearance, and paid Darington to help sell the tale. A man that devoted to his reputation, that ruthless, might do anything to Cecilia should he find her.

"What will you do once he's gone?" Cecilia turned back to him. The sunlight reddened her white-blonde hair.

"I shall set you up in the Greydrake home, for a start, or in your own, if you prefer. You'll be the dowager marchioness."

She laughed. "A dowager at twenty-two. I shall feel so old."

"You won't be. I'm sure you won't lack for suitors, if you wish a new life."

"I don't know. What if..." She twisted her hands in her lap. "I didn't choose your father, mine did, but I didn't protest. The marquess seemed mysterious and handsome. Aloof, yes, but that was all." She turned her hands over, palms up. "I'm obviously not a good judge of men."

"You were sixteen. I'm sure you'll do better now." He grinned. "Besides, I know every rake in London. If one dares approach you, my dear step-mama, I'll shoot him."

"That's very sweet of you." She studied him. "You haven't answered my question, though. I meant, what will you do for yourself, not for me."

"That depends on the next score of days." His smile evaporated. "The old bastard says I must marry by then, so he can approve my bride, or he will sign everything over to Madelina."

"She's only sixteen."

"Lethbridge will be her guardian."

Cecilia frowned. "That's not good. I don't trust that man. No one could work for your father for as long as he has and be honest."

"I agree, so I must wed, and quickly." For Madelina's sake, Cecilia's, his own, and his plans to help keep other women from ending up like his mother. For those, he needed the marquess's money. He would find justice in using the old man's hoard to aid the downtrodden of London.

"So you must wed." She pursed her lips, thinking. "Surely there's someone you've noticed? Someone who intrigues you?"

Darington's daughter, as painted by his letters, flittered through William's mind. "It wouldn't matter. The old bastard had Lethbridge draw up a list."

Cecilia nodded, compassion in her eyes. "Of course he did. Why leave the choice of your wife to you?" She sighed, then cast off her moment of gloom like tossing off a cloak. "Will I see you at breakfast? I finished the latest Walter Scott. We might exchange thoughts on it."

He shook his head. "I can't give the appearance of staying here all night. The marquess is suspicious I love my mistress. I'm sure to be followed and the hours I remain reported."

"Shall we change out the servants and choose a new name again?"

"Likely, but that would necessitate another meeting with Lethbridge. Besides, I'm fond of Chastity. I enjoy the irony."

"So long as you feel it's safe." Her smile brightened. "I was thinking Valentina for next time."

He shook his head, amused. "You can't pull off Italian, and there won't be a next time. The old man will die soon."

"We can only pray you're right," she said fervently.

William rose and bowed. "Now, if you'll excuse me, I want to check the streets."

"You will be careful, won't you? You know I enjoy practicing my surgical skills, putting all my study to test, but last time you gave me a worry. That knife would have killed you if it hadn't hit your rib."

"But it did hit my rib, and that was nothing but a small scrape. A minor inconvenience. You stitched it up beautifully."

"Yes, well, I get plenty of practice. Has it occurred to you that you may not be very good at what you're doing, with how often you're injured?"

William put his hands to his heart, affecting a hurt expression. "You wound me deeper than any blade."

Her expression softened. "I don't want anything to happen to you."

"Yet you never tell me not to go." He wouldn't have listened, but he wouldn't have blamed her.

"I don't know why you do it, William, but I can tell you must." Her smile returned. "Besides, I do know you're quite good. I was only cossetting you. Someone must, and I am your stepmother."

"And I appreciate it very much, step-mama dearest."

"When you return, would you like me to yell and scream and rail against you marrying, so the servants can hear?"

"We can do it another time. It's not worth waiting up for. Will you lock the doors?" It wouldn't do for a servant to come by and find no one in a compromising position.

She nodded. "Happy hunting."

Using the adjoining door, he entered her bedroom, ignoring the door to his own. A key unlocked a compartment hidden in the heavy headboard. William slid out a set of common garb, a wide brimmed hat, and the scarf that covered the lower half of his face. After changing attire, he crossed to her dressing table and released the secret drawer beneath it, large enough to hold a knife, pistol and powder. He loaded the pistol and put it through his belt, then slipped the knife into a boot.

A glance showed it was dark now, night coming quickly in the gathering London fog. William doused the candles and opened the doors of the Juliet balcony. A blur in the dark, he climbed onto the railing and jumped upward. He easily caught the edge of the roof and pulled himself up. The marquess's men watched the house from the street, so he kept low as he ran along the garden-side of the roof. A short five-foot jump carried him to the next roof over, and the next.

The rooftops grew lower and closer together as William made his way into the poorest section of London. From his vantage point above, he patrolled the streets he and his mother had called home for a decade. Good people lived there. People who were doing their best to have peaceful, decent lives and feed their children. They were easy targets for the worst sorts of opportunists, for the bulk of the city couldn't be bothered to right their misfortunes.

The night seemed peaceful. William was pleased. He would finish his rounds and return to Cecilia. If she was awake, they could discuss Walter Scott's latest work before he left. He knew she was starved for company, locked in that house nearly alone, with servants she could never fully trust.

He didn't need to watch over the borough throughout the dark hours. Soon, decent folk would be abed. William had no care for what those who lurked on the streets in the wee hours visited upon each other. They weren't his concern.

He was returning to Cecilia's when a furtive movement caught his eye. A woman, worn coat fastened tight and bonnet pulled low, hurried down the street. Her gaze darted, trying to be everywhere. The way she clutched her hands to her chest bespoke of someone in possession of more money than they were accustomed to, and afraid of losing it. William slipped along the rooftops, careful to keep her in sight.

She didn't see the man until he slithered from an alley into her path. She stopped with a gasp, then made to go around him. He sidestepped into her path.

"Where are you going so late, Miss?" His voice was rough, words slurred.

"To see the doctor. There's sickness in my house."

She said it as if it might stop him. William knew better. This man's type was already dying. William lowered himself from the roof into the shadows behind the man. He dropped the final few feet, silent.

"What've you got there?" The would-be robber reached for her clutched hands.

"No. It's for my girl." She didn't yell, likely aware that could attract as much unwanted notice as help.

"Yeah? It's for my drink now. Give it here."

William drew his pistol, took two steps, and pressed the weapon to the back of the man's head. "If she gives you that purse, it will be the last thing you ever put your hands on."

The woman gasped.

The man whirled and swung at William. He dodged back.

"Why if it isn't Lord Lefthook, ruining a man's fun." The robber drove his fist toward William's jaw.

William dodged again. "I see my reputation precedes me."

"Aye, and I know you won't use that pistol." The words were accompanied by a wild swing.

William ducked. He stuffed the pistol into his belt. He preferred not to kill. He brought up his fists. "You're correct. I won't use it, unless I must."

"You saying I'm not worth shooting?"

"Probably not. Gun powder isn't cheap."

The man dove forward, fists swinging wildly. William ducked under the flailing blows. He came up close enough to smell the man's rancid breath. He slammed both arms out, throwing the robber's arms wide. The man staggered back. William cocked his arm. A single blow sent the man flying. He landed on his back and skidded across the cobblestones toward the woman. She stepped aside as the limp form slid until the man's head checked up against the rough stone of a building.

Wide eyes turned to William. "Lord Lefthook?" she whispered.

"At your service." William moved to stand before her. He bowed. "You're walking the streets rather late, Miss."

"Missus," she said quickly. "Missus Banke. I know, my lord, but my daughter is sick. I can't go in the day on account of I had to work, and I had to try to feed her before I could come out."

He doubted she'd fed herself. "The doctor won't be in at this time of night."

She looked about, forlorn. She was frail, and young. "I thought an extra penny might wake him."

William knew the old charlatan, who claimed to be a doctor. A penny might wake him, but he would do her child no good. "You've been skipping meals to save?"

Her eyes grew rounder. She gave a shaky nod.

"I take it there's no Mister Banke?" Beside them, the robber groaned. Eyes still on the woman, William kicked him in the ribs.

"How do you know?" she asked.

"A guess." Her story was a common one. Men died, they deserted their families, they went to war and didn't return. They beat their eldest son to death for fearing horses, causing a mother to run off with her remaining child and be declared a mad murderess. It was the dark side of life. If Mrs. Banke had a husband, she wouldn't be so thin, or made to walk the streets at night because missing a day of work would mean no food for her daughter. His mother had lived like this for years to keep him from the marquess.

William handed her a card. It was monogramed with Lord Lefthook's initials. "Take this to the doctor on Amber Street. He will help you. He may need to return with you to examine your daughter. It's safe to let him."

Her hand shook as she took the card. "I can't pay him. He's too fine."

He wasn't fine by London standards, but William knew him to be honest and good at his craft. They had an ongoing association, and a shared desire to alleviate the suffering in their city. "He'll accept that card in payment. He'll also have some coin for you, so you are to go during the day. He won't be open at night," he added, in case she thought to risk herself again and keep the extra coin.

"Thank you, my lord," she stammered. "I never thought to see you with my own eyes. I wasn't sure you were real."

"You can best thank me by not putting yourself in such danger again. I am not everywhere."

"Yes, my lord."

"You can see yourself home?"

"Yes, my lord. Thank you." She bobbed an awkward curtsy and hurried back the way she'd come.

William nudged the would-be robber with his foot. The man groaned. William dropped a couple coins on his chest as his eyes opened. "You look like you could use a drink, friend," he said, before disappearing into the darkness to make sure Mrs. Banke got home.

CHAPTER FOUR

Lanora took in the dwindling line with satisfaction. After three days in the small building on the back of the church, she'd finally handed out enough bread that people had better activities for their time than waiting for it. Sadly, in a few more days they would be willing to line up again, but for now they and their families were fed. She wished she could offer meat as well, but it wasn't practical to distribute.

Perhaps meat pies, she mused. Grace would know what was best. Lanora should likewise look into procuring fruit. As she handed out the last few loaves of bread, she pictured the look on Grace's face at the suggestion of a trip to the wharfs to bargain for fruit.

"No thank you, Missus," the woman standing before her said.

Lanora blinked. "You don't want bread?"

The woman, not much older than Lanora and too frail to be turning down food, shook her head. "I was wanting to ask a favor of you, Missus." She leaned close. "In private."

Lanora looked down the line. "Well, I've only a few dozen more loaves, and I count about twenty people in line. If you take some to the end of the line, I'll be free to speak with you sooner."

The woman nodded. Clean enough hands scooped up an armful of loaves. She scuttled away as Lanora resumed passing out bread. The murmurs and suspicious looks ended as soon as the young woman began handing out what she carried.

By the time the line was gone, Lanora had only four loaves remaining. Those she took outside, where she knew urchins lurked. They were too afraid to enter, as parentless children were often rounded up and put into orphanages. Hungry eyes watched her lay the loaves on the bottom step and walk away, gesturing for the woman to follow. Trying to nourish the urchins was like feeding feral cats. They suspected every kindness of being a trap.

The woman fell in stride with her as they passed from the churchyard to the narrow street, her gaze shifted past Lanora's shoulder. "Them boys belong in an orphanage, or a workhouse."

"That's hardly my trouble," Lanora said. "I aim only to give them a respite from hunger."

The woman chewed on her lip. "Where are we going?"

"I'm going to visit the foreman in charge of the new home for women, Mr. Finch. May I assume speaking while we walk is private enough?" The woman seemed harmless, but Lanora wasn't about to go off alone with her. She wasn't the fool Grace worried she was.

"Are they really building a place for women whose menfolk have abandoned them and their babes?" The woman sounded wistful.

"They are." At least, if Lanora had any say, they were. "Progress should never have stopped. Is that what you wished to speak with me about, Miss?"

"Missus Banke. I'm a widow, like you, Missus."

Lanora smoothed her dull grey skirt. She could play a role, but wasn't an accomplished dissembler. She found it best to bring a falsehood into being quickly and let rumor carry it through. If she had to lie to the face of each person, she wouldn't succeed in her ruse. "And do you have children, Mrs. Banke?"

"A daughter. It's somewhat on account of her I need the favor."

Lanora wished she'd saved some of the bread. The woman would ask for money now, for her sick child, who may or may not exist. Likely, Mrs. Banke thought turning down the bread would make her plea seem more honest, but Lanora never dispensed coin. Only food, lessons or work that might be done to earn money.

She stopped and motioned for Mrs. Banke to step to the side of the roughly cobbled street, where they could speak without blocking passing traffic. "I don't have any coin. I will return with more food in a few days." The woman hardly had enough meat on her to last a few days, but Lanora hadn't forced her to give up her loaf.

Mrs. Banke shook her head. "I'm not asking for a handout, Missus." She sounded offended. "I need a favor."

Lanora looked down to hide her surprise, suitably chastened. "What favor?"

"They say you can write, and read and all."

"I can."

"I got a story about Lord Lefthook for the paper. They pay for stories."

Lanora's brows shot up. "You met Lord Lefthook?"

The woman smiled, her head bobbing up and down in confirmation. "I did, and I want to sell my story to them papers, but I know better than to go there." Her words bubbled out. "The boys, like the ones you left the bread for, they watch the papers. Anyone sees me in there, they'll know I got paid. They'll rob me. You're always here helping people. I want you to get my money for me and no one the wiser."

"So, you want me to take down your story and deliver it to the paper, then bring back your payment?" Lanora didn't know if she was more amused or surprised. "Perhaps I could simply remember it for you?"

"You'll do it, then?" Her eyes darted about again, but the few passers-by seemed disinterested. "I don't know anyone else I can ask, you see, who won't take any, or spread my name."

What a sad thing that said about this woman's life. "You trust me so much, when we've never met before?"

The woman looked her up and down. "You bring all that food, and you're finer than you pretend. I can hear it when you talk. You won't be tempted by what the papers'll pay me."

Lanora frowned. Perhaps Grace was right. Mrs. Smith might not be the foolproof costume Lanora thought. "Did you really meet Lord Lefthook? Do you have proof?"

The woman pulled out a card and extended it to Lanora. It was a fine make. A gentleman's card. On it were Lord Lefthook's initials. She turned it over, but found nothing.

"You can take that to the papers as proof," Mrs. Banke said. "They seen those before."

"You don't need it?" Lanora ran her fingers over the monogram.

"I already shown it to the doctor. He knows me now."

Lanora tucked the card away. "Doctor?"

Mrs. Banke's head bobbed again. "I was on my way to see a doctor, for my girl, when some fellow who weren't no gentleman tried to take the coin I'd saved for the medicine. Lord Lefthook appears, and he lays the fellow out with one swing."

To Lanora's amusement, Mrs. Banke mimicked a punch, much as Grace had.

"But that's not all." Mrs. Banke lowered her voice. "He gave me that card and said I was to go to another doctor, one what's much finer than I could ever afford, and Lord Lefthook has it all paid for, the visits and the medicine." Her voice dropped to the barest whisper. "And the doctor gave me money so as I don't have to work this week, so I can care for my girl."

Lanora stared at Mrs. Banke. Lord Lefthook sounded too good to be true. "And they didn't ask for anything, Lord Lefthook or the doctor?"

Mrs. Banke shook her head vigorously. "Not a thing, and Doctor Carter gave me tonic for my girl. She doesn't like how it tastes, she says, but she's doing better already."

"I'm pleased to hear that," Lanora said. "So, you would like me to trade your story to the *Times* for coin?"

"It would be a help to me, Missus, but don't give them my name or nothing."

"Certainly not."

"And don't give them the whole story till they pay. Those writers can be sneaky, I hear. Learning to write does that to a brain, makes it cunning." She cast Lanora a startled look. "Meaning no offense, Missus."

"I took none." Lanora frowned. "If the boys watch the papers, as you said, and would rob you, won't I endanger myself by going in and then returning here?"

Mrs. Banke chuckled. "Nah. No one would lay a finger on you, Missus. Half the borough would stone them on account of you bring us food. The other half would because robbing a gentlewoman will bring the Runners. No one wants that kind of trouble round here."

Lanora nodded. Though she was mostly convinced, she would send Grace, who never set foot in the shadier parts of London. That should be safe enough for all concerned and Grace would be overjoyed to go to the *Times* with another story of how valiant Lefthook was. "I'll bring the money when I hand out bread, but if I don't see you, I'll leave it with the doctor. You said his name is Carter?" She would also attempt to learn more about Lord Lefthook, who obviously associated with the man.

"Doctor Carter, on Amber." Mrs. Banke attempted a curtsey. "Thank you, Missus."

Lanora watched Mrs. Banke walk away, torn. She'd meant to hunt down the foreman for the new home for women again. She wished to know why work still hadn't resumed.

If only Lanora could write to Mr. Darington, she might ask him about the work, instead of hunting for the foreman, but she couldn't. It wouldn't be proper, even if he was in Egypt. She'd considered writing his solicitor, for she knew the man's name and address. She'd looked into him once, when her father's old man of business passed and she was made to research another for him. Mr. Lethbridge was known to be good. Her father had refused him, though, saying Mr. Darington didn't speak very highly of him. It was that disparagement that made her hesitate in approaching him.

She'd written to her father about the money again, but he'd never replied. He was like that with letters. When she was young, she'd written him weekly, and still often did. He rarely replied. She had no way of knowing if he had received her inquiry, all the way in Egypt, nor had she any reason to think he'd answer. Even if he did, with Egypt across all of Europe and two seas, getting news to and from there was slow.

Not that Mrs. Smith's words to the foreman would amount to any change, even assuming she could locate the man. She'd already spoken to him several times, to no avail. Resolved, she altered her course. It wasn't a long walk to Dr. Carter's on Amber.

CHAPTER FIVE

William slipped from the low rooftop as Mrs. Smith drew away. He'd come to the borough to assure himself Mrs. Banke was using the resources he'd provided to care for her child, and followed her to the back of the church where food was being dispensed. When she left in the company of the Widow Smith, his interest was well and truly piqued.

He knew Mrs. Smith by reputation. A widow who used her late husband's money to buy food for the poor. She was new to London, or at least to charity work. The borough was rather taken with her. William had assumed the infatuation sprang from gratitude.

Though the hair under her bonnet was a dusty grey, as was her frumpy garb, and spectacles perched on her nose, she moved with the grace of a young woman. Not just young, but polished. Her long-fingered hands also bespoke of sophistication. When she looked up and down the street, even her dowdy ensemble couldn't hide a slender, elegant neck.

Most intriguing of all was the unshakable sense that he was acquainted with her. That's what kept him following her, instead of Mrs. Banke. It was the reason he was determined to catch a real look at the face under the low bonnet and spectacles. Besides, he'd managed to hear enough of their conversation to assure himself on Mrs. Banke's and her daughter's accounts.

Normally, dressed in common workman garb and a solid coating of dust, William would have approached the widow and struck up a conversation. Today, he meandered along behind her, keeping his distance. He desired to place her, and couldn't risk that she might place him.

He followed her to Dr. Carter's, amusement and curiosity growing. So, she wished to learn more about Lord Lefthook. She wouldn't glean anything from Carter. He knew nothing. To the doctor, Lefthook was a mysterious figure who communicated only in writing. Women's writing, to be more precise, since Cecilia penned all of Lefthook's letters. William couldn't risk that anyone might recognize his hand, and he and Carter had attended university together. The doctor was a nobleman's younger son, and a good man.

William purchased a meat pie and lingered across the street from Carter's, eating slowly as he waited for Mrs. Smith to leave. He was impressed with the length of time the lady remained within. It showed a perseverance he didn't ascribe to most females.

When she did come stomping out, green eyes hot with frustration, William nearly dropped the remainder of his meal. He did drop his head and used the pie to hide his face, and thanked God he hadn't taken his usual tact of believing no one who knew him could possibly frequent the poorest part of London. Of all the women in the world, not for a moment had William Greydrake guessed that Mrs. Smith was in truth Lady Lanora Hadler, daughter of the Duke of Solworth.

William turned his back on Lady Lanora as angry strides carried her up the street. He forced his feet to move, returning the way they'd come. Lingering outside Carter's wasn't completely safe. In his workman's garb, William was generally invisible to the gentry, but Carter was of a sympathetic sort. He might actually look at a poor man's face.

As, apparently, would Lady Lanora. William's brain fumbled to catch up with the idea. Contributing to charities. Discussing them over tea. That's what ladies did. They did not don the persona of a greying widow, enter the less savory parts of London alone, and pass out bread. Further, William knew it wasn't a daring jaunt, a fluke born of the boredom of the leisure class. Mrs. Smith had been assisting the poor for... He nearly missed a step. Mrs. Smith had been assisting the poor since the start of the London season.

Why? He looked back, but the church was streets away. Why would one of London's most prized jewels secretly spend her days in the back of a ramshackle church in the worst part of town, handing out food?

Did the borough know who she was? He shook his head. They couldn't, or the boys would have told him. Then, they were less forthcoming about Mrs. Smith than most topics. William had assumed there was little to tell, and the urchins had no interest in an aging do-gooder. Now, he wasn't so sure.

He shook his head in an effort to press the riddle of Lady Lanora from his mind. He had a second mission that day, after checking on Mrs. Banke, and he'd best see to it before the midday meal was past. His garb and general state of grubbiness marked him as a bricklayer for a purpose other than anonymity.

A few casual conversations later found William at the tavern the foreman in charge of the women's home, Mr. Finch, was known to patronize. It was clean, as far as such places went, with rushes on the floor no more than a week old. The aroma and number of patrons argued for good fare.

Finch sat alone at a table near the middle of the floor. He was bent over a gravy-slathered pie, mug of ale close at hand. A powerfully built man who still had all his teeth, which marked him as well fed and likely good in a fight.

William strode to the table where Finch sat and snagged an empty chair. He settled into it at the foreman's table. "By your leave?" he said, slipping into an accent learned in ten years of living in the borough.

"Seems you're already sitting." Finch took a swig of ale, washing down the food that obstructed his words, then shoved in more.

"I hear you're the man to talk to for work."

"Guess so."

"Need a bricklayer?"

"When the work starts back up I could use you," Finch said around a fatty bite of what William assumed was horse.

"Works not going? I heard tell it had begun again."

Finch turned his head and spat. "So did I, but the money didn't come. I passed on another job for this. Said that famous Darington fellow, always making talk for his exploring, put up the funds. Thought for sure it'd be a good year for me. Now, I got workers I can't pay, piles of supplies attracting thieves, and no funds coming in."

William took in the man's well-fed state again. He didn't look to be in need of coin. "Rich folk," he grumbled. "Likely forgot he wanted it built."

"Well, he'd best remember soon."

"I'll leave you to it." William stood. He would have to ask the boys for more on this man. Finch ate well for someone with unpaid workers hounding him. Could he have pocketed Darington's money, thinking a man in Egypt would have little recourse in London?

"Check back in a week," Finch said. He took another swig. "Can always use a bricklayer."

William tipped his cap, then left. Darington had not forgotten about the funds. His last letter stipulated they'd been requested. If Darington said it, William knew it to be true.

He headed into an alleyway and donned the scarf he used to cover his face. Identity better hidden, he found a group of street urchins and put out the word he would pay for the location of Finch's lodgings.

That done, he set out for one of the shadier clubs in London. Lord William often let the marquess's men follow him there. They would wait outside for hours, never knowing he rented a private room on the top floor where Lord Lefthook came and went via the window.

William had been both pleased and surprised when Darington sent word he was funding the building for displaced women. A longtime dream of William's, a safe place for women who found themselves with a child but no man, he'd thought the building would need to wait until the marquess died. It was doubly satisfying to have the funds come from the man the marquess had paid off to explain William's ten-year absence from society. William preferred to imagine Darington using that exact payment, in essence turning the marquess's money into a place of safety for those he was apt to mistreat.

William didn't know the nature of the relationship shared by Darington and the marquess. At first, he'd been suspicious of the archaeologist. The marquess had supplied the man with an unknown sum to convince the world William was in Egypt from age four to fourteen, having been sent there upon the death of his brother. It would never do for society to know William had, in fact, grown up in the poorest part of London, the only place his mother could find refuge for them.

Near the club, William ducked into an alley, ignoring the acrid smell. A glance revealed him to be unobserved. A rough stone wall and a slight excursion of strength brought him to a rooftop. Keeping to the back sides of the buildings, he angled toward the short jump that would take him through the window of the club.

William was at home on the streets and rooftops of London, and with the gravely cadence of the poor Londoner's speech. It was a hard life. It made a man strong, but aged him quickly. There was rarely assurance, or even hope, of a better tomorrow.

Yet there was a realness to this life, a sense of being alive, that was absent in the higher echelons. A ballroom could be only so invigorating. He could muster only so much concern for whether Lady So-and-So had been seen in the park with Lord Such-and-Such, her gloves in her lap instead of encasing her fingers. Even gambling and boxing held only a hint of the veracity of life in the borough.

He came to the edge of the roof. It was less than a four-foot jump across a narrow alley to the window, which remained open. He stared into that dark rectangle, thinking of the girl inside. She never asked where he went, or why he changed into workmen's garb. She took as payment a small amount of coin and this time to herself, when her master thought she was pleasing him. That was more than enough to buy her loyalty, her silence.

That was part of the darker side, the sharp edge to life gifted by the street. Any freedom was a myth, and life was vivid only because it balanced so nearly with death. William knew he was blessed to be able to look back at his time there, seen through the eyes of youth, with any longing. The truth was, poverty was an indominable weight that stole life and crushed all hope.

A weight that, apparently, Lady Lanora sought to alleviate. Seeing her attempts to blend into the world of the borough evoked painful memories of his mother. As a boy of four, he'd adapted, but his mother never had. She tried, desperately. She never wished to attract attention. All she wanted was the job she took as a washwoman, food for them, and a bit of time in the evenings to teach William.

He conjured up a vision of her long, yellow hair tied back. He could hear her nearly flawless Italian, her French. He spoke both with the accent she'd taught him, a lingering memory of her in each word. He remembered learning his letters, penmanship practiced in charcoal on a slate, and figures.

William had done his part. He'd quickly learned to beg with the other boys, then moved on to fetching and carrying. He'd done odd jobs for a baker, and an innkeeper. His greatest skill, though, was fighting for money.

His mother repeatedly begged him not to. As with many boy, he believed he knew better than she did, and he did it regardless. He recalled her tears the night he stumbled home with both eyes swelling shut, a fat purse of pennies clutched in his hands.

Then she fell ill. It was a cough. It seemed like little, but grew worse. Always thin, she was soon frail. When delirium overtook her and the tonics he could afford didn't help, William sought out the marquess.

William found him at Whites, and held the man's horse until he came out. There was never any doubt in the marquess's eyes. He knew William on sight. If the welcome was cold, William attributed it to the marquess's shock.

Shocking to William was his young sister, and his stepmother. They believed the same story as the rest of the *ton*. William's mother went mad, murdered his brother Charles, then was locked up and died. William, too distressing to look upon, was sent away. The marquess told William the tale when he brought him to the Westlock family home.

It was the first time William heard the lie. The new addition to the deception, created to explain William's return, was that William had returned from Egypt, where he'd been these ten years. That explained his oddities. No one dared ask the marquess why he hadn't told the world where he'd sent his son until after William reappeared.

After securing William in the Westlock townhouse, the marquess went to William's mother. Instead of helping her, he had her jailed. William, allowed to see her after much pleading, found her nearly dead, but lucid.

"Do whatever your father asks," she'd whispered.

She'd lain on a cot, her face turned toward the bars. The guard who'd left William to speak with her hadn't opened the cell. William had no way to reach her.

"I don't understand. Why are you locked in here? Where are the doctors?" William had worked hard not to cry, feeling himself too grown at fourteen to do so.

"Do you know why we left your father?" Her voice was soft.

William leaned his forehead into the bars. "You never said."

"Do you remember Charlie? Your brother?"

He nodded, the marquess's words about his mother murdering Charles loud in his head. He couldn't believe it of her, didn't wish to hear her confess it.

"Your father beat him to death. Charlie was afraid of horses. Your father swore that no son of his would have any weakness in him."

William closed his eyes as he'd done twelve years ago, when he'd learned the truth. He'd turned his mother over to a man who beat his son to death. William hadn't saved her.

"William," he heard her gentle voice in his head, "I'm dying. You did not do this to me. You must live with him now. Be what he wishes you to be. Remember Charlie." She'd let out a long sigh and turned her face away. "Remember me."

He had cried then. He couldn't restrain himself. Soon, the guard reappeared. William never saw his mother again.

The marquess's second marriage remained a legal bond. Madelina's mother never knew her husband was a bigamist, their marriage never legal. They'd had the semblance of a happy family for a year, during which William exchanged letters with Darington and learned about his imagined time in Egypt. Then William's stepmother had her accident, and little Madalina was sent to a boarding school.

William opened his eyes and scanned for the lowering sun through the London haze. Even the marquess's depraved men wouldn't imagine he could amuse himself with a cheap doxy for much longer tonight. He'd wallowed in memories long enough. Doing so did him no good, only fueled anguish.

He must press the past back into its place. He had to go in and change, then return to the world of the *ton*. He had a ball to attend. One where he would, for the first time, seek out a dance with one of the women on Lethbridge's list, the intriguing Lady Lanora Hadler.

CHAPTER SIX

Lanora winced as Grace tugged at her laces and muttered to herself.

"No one can understand you, you realize?" Lanora snapped.

"I said, I cannot believe you were so late." Grace's hands stilled. She looked up to meet Lanora's eyes in the mirror. "You know how long it takes to get the powder out of your hair. It'll take all evening to clean up this room, while you flitter the night away dancing. If you hadn't brought me such a marvelous story and Lord Lefthook's card, I should never forgive you."

"You know I'd have you with me tonight if I could." Lanora pulled a face. "The *ton* and their snobbery. They're ridiculous. Simply because you weren't born into a certain family, you cannot attend their dances?"

Grace's expression softened. "This isn't your father's estate in the country, Lanora, where you can set the rules. I know you would let us all dance if you could, though Cook would be terrible at it." She giggled.

"It's their loss. You, at least, would provide interesting conversation. The young women I'll spend my evening surrounded by care only for hemlines and the weather."

"And Lord Lefthook." Grace smiled. "You could tell them your new story. You'd be a hit."

"I most certainly cannot tell them that." Lanora shook her head. The gems arranged in her black hair glinted in the mirror. "Not before it's in the paper. I don't want to be associated with the man."

"Well, I can't go to the paper until tomorrow." Grace let out a contented sigh. "In two days, this new feat of Lord Lefthook's will be all the talk, but I knew about it first."

Lanora pointed out that at least five people, likely more, knew before Grace. "Perhaps we should invent a title for you, or simply a gentrified papa. If I introduce you around town as my distant cousin and special friend, no one will question you. I'm the daughter of a duke. They must take my word if I say you're a gentlewoman."

Grace returned to her lacing. "Don't you dare. We have enough trouble with Mrs. Smith. I am not becoming someone else, as well. I'm quite happy to be your maid."

"And friend," Lanora said firmly.

Grace nodded. "Certainly, we're friends. My mama raised you with me, in that giant fortress your papa calls a house. Why he never got you a proper nanny after your grandfather died, or even before, I'll never know."

"I daresay he simply forgot." Lanora's tone was wistful. "Who would remind him? I don't believe he even read my letters when I was a child, he missed Mama so much. Not that I could write very well, or had anything to say." Not that he seemed to read most of them now, though she wrote almost weekly.

Lanora could see Grace's pursed lips in the mirror. She knew her friend was trying to contain one of her most worn rants. For all Grace claimed they were practically sisters, she still saw a difference in their station. She resented Lanora being raised more as a member of the staff than as a duke's daughter. In Grace's view, it simply wasn't right.

Lanora didn't resent it one bit. What need had she for needlepoint or water colors? She could play and sing to brighten their days and evenings. She'd learned from her father's books, as well. She could read and write in Latin, Greek, French and Italian, though she didn't speak any of the four. She knew her figures well enough to get by. Her knowledge of geography, history and politics was excellent.

She'd also learned to ride, shoot and pick locks. She'd attempted Egyptian, but fell short. In her younger mind, she'd believed her father would appreciate her efforts and send for her. She wanted to be the perfect addition to his archeological team. Then, he would keep her by his side and they would be a family.

Lanora suppressed a sigh. She knew now he would never send for her, no matter how much she learned. So here she was, not possessing all the skills she should to be a lady, though she'd never admit as much to the world. No one would ever know, of course, that she couldn't paint, stitch prettily or draw, so the skills mattered little.

Dancing was a greater difficulty. Lanora was accomplished at the country reels she and the staff enjoyed. London dances were more complex, though. Most, she could pick up from watching, for they were adaptations on what she knew. The new dance, the waltz, was confounding. Fortunately, one frosty glance and an easily spread rumor of her disdain for the scandalous activity kept any gentleman from daring to waltz with her.

"Arms out," Grace said.

Lanora complied, and Grace fitted another layer over her. "It really would be nice to have you with me to talk to."

"You'll have your aunt."

Lanora groaned. "Aunt Edith will only talk about one thing."

"You love her terriers."

"I do, but there's the carriage ride over, the whole evening, and the ride back. How many hours would you want to speak about who treed a squirrel, or the upcoming litter, or the arguments for and opposed to letting their hair grow down over their eyes, based on breed, of course?"

"I thought dogs had fur, not hair, and why would you allow it to grow down over their eyes?"

Lanora closed hers. "No. I am not permitting the discussion of terriers to commence already."

"You began it."

She popped her eyes open and narrowed them at Grace.

"Well, you did." Grace tugged at Lanora's pale sage green gown to ensure it draped properly. "Now get your slippers, the matching ones this time. I'll go see if your aunt is ready. No sense you lingering in the foyer while she kisses two dozen pups goodbye."

Lanora went to dig in her wardrobe as Grace departed. She pulled out cream slippers that would go perfectly well, and a pair that seemed more blue than green. Pale pink, light yellow and lavender followed. Her eyes went back to the cream, discarded on the floor beside her. Grace would never know.

"For goodness sake, Lanora, they're on the upper shelf with the other new sets. Remember?" Grace appeared around the wardrobe door, reaching to lift down slippers that matched the gown to perfection.

Lanora took them to the bed to sit while she put them on. "This is silly. All that money on slippers that are worn what, a handful of times at most? Think of all the people that would feed."

"Think of all the people they did feed, to bring the materials and fashion them into footwear for you."

Lanora stood and wiggled her toes in the slippers. "A cream pair would match most every gown here." She gestured to the pastel montage. "It isn't as if I'm permitted to wear any interesting colors." None that would actually look good with her unrelentingly black hair.

"I thought we agreed you know nothing about fashion and it should be left to me." Grace's gaze took in the scattered slippers. "I'll give the old pairs to the poor, if you like, but now you must go. Your aunt is waiting in the carriage."

Lanora squared her shoulders and smoothed all expression from her face. "Hopefully, we won't be late."

"Hopefully, you will. Have a lovely time. Steal a kiss with a charming gentleman for me."

That cracked Lanora's façade. She laughed as she headed for the staircase, but regained composure by the time she reached the bottom. Steal a kiss indeed. Even if she encountered a gentleman who inspired the notion, she was much too reasonable to do any such thing.

The night was cool as she descended the steps and let a footman hand her into the carriage. She settled across from her aunt, who wore a billowing gown that was older than Lanora. Two terriers sprawled on the floor of the carriage. They would make nice foot warmers on the ride home. A third sat beside Aunt Edith, nose turned toward the outside world.

"You look pretty tonight, dear," Aunt Edith said.

"Thank you, Aunt. You do as well."

Her aunt cackled. "Do you hear that, Fetcher, my niece just called me pretty." She patted the rough coat of the terrier beside her. "I'm no prettier than Fetcher here, but you're kind to say it."

"Fetcher is adorable." Lanora smiled at the scruffy blond dog. "You know, in a flea-bitten, grubby, unkempt sort of way."

Aunt Edith laughed anew. She slapped her knee, releasing a puff of dust from the gown. "You find a gentleman who appreciates you calling your old aunt flea-bitten and you'll have a winner, girl."

Lanora's smile vanished. "I don't wish to find a gentleman. Surely you've gathered that? I will be like you. You had a husband for only a day, and you're the happiest woman I know."

Aunt Edith shook her grey head. "I was fortunate enough to wed a dying man, and to have a brother. You have no one. The world knows your father's left everything to you but his title and the one entailed estate. Think of your home and all your love, girl. Who will care for the tenants when your father and you are gone? You've got to get yourself with child, then raise that child to love those things you love. Otherwise, the Solworth properties will fall into bits and pieces and who knows what will become of all those beholden to you?"

Lanora leaned back in her seat, dismayed. She'd never thought of her life in those terms. Was that the sort of thing a man said to his son, to cause him to marry? It was a compelling argument.

"It's not fair," she whispered.

"I daresay it isn't." Aunt Edith patted Fetcher on the head. "Not fair you haven't a brother, or lost your mama, or never see your father, but you've a good head on you, girl. You'll see it all come right."

"But I don't want a gentleman," Lanora said. "Someone to own what is mine, order me about and tell me who my friends may be. I want to be free, like you, or Queen Elizabeth."

"You hear that, Fletcher? Now I'm akin to the Virgin Queen." Aunt Edith chuckled. "Give it some thought, girl. This is your first season and you've hardly eighteen years to your name. You may find, if you don't glower at them so, a gentleman worth marrying. Perhaps he's one of the handful who still dares dance with you. You can hope so, since you've scared the others away."

Lanora made the rest of the journey in silence, contemplating her aunt's words. She knew only a small portion of the Solworth estate must be passed to a male heir, in this case, a cousin. She knew she would receive the remainder. Her aunt was correct, though. Lanora had never thought about what would happen to everyone she cared for once she was gone. Her father never spoke of such things. Should she write to him for his thoughts? It seemed the sort of letter he would conveniently claim never reached him in Egypt.

The carriage turned down a wide cobbled drive. They were late enough to have avoided the initial press, and in short order came to a halt before a splendidly lit home. It was a new construction, large by London standards, near the edge of town. Statues adorned the corners, and lurked on the roof high above, over the vast entry door.

Lanora allowed their footman to hand her down. She offered him a murmur of thanks before firming her expression into frostiness. Her aunt may be correct, but the issue required lengthier contemplation than a carriage ride. Lanora would need to appear approachable but once to ruin months of work. Before she permitted that to happen, she must think longer on the dilemma Aunt Edith had set before her.

"Now, you lot be good and help guard the carriage," Aunt Edith said behind Lanora. "You know you can't come with me. I'll sneak you back some fancy fare."

While her aunt went through her goodbyes, Lanora amused herself by picturing the fun of bringing the scruffy little miscreants inside with them. They would steal the spread. They would trip dancers and leave fur imbedded in finely upholstered chairs, to end up on ladies' gowns. It would be a delightful distraction from a tedious evening of staring down gentlemen until they gave up trying to persuade her to dance.

Lanora waited while her aunt clambered down from the carriage unassisted, then followed her into the crowded, noise-and-light-filled home. Fine material and chatter abounded, the gentlemen clad in dark and the ladies in light. The high ceilings were alive with idyllic country scenes. The clamor of color that swam above nearly outshone the sea of black tailcoats and bouquet of gowns below.

Proper greetings were exchanged with their hosts. Aunt Edith set a straight line toward the few old friends she had in London. As they pressed through the hot sea of guests, Lanora considered sneaking away. She wished to be alone with the thoughts her aunt's words stirred in her head.

As they drew near the flock of older women, Lanora realized there was a rooster among the hens, though an elegantly clad one. He stood at least a foot taller than the mamas and aunts clustered around him. His back was to her, but she recognized the unruly mane and the indolent stance. If those clues weren't enough, the breathless quality to the giggles he was enticing spoke volumes. Lord William Greydrake, future Marquess of Westlock.

Lanora's steps faltered. The terrace or perhaps the library would be preferable to Lord William's rakishness, so disappointingly at odds with her hopes for a man raised by her father's friend, Mr. Darington, in the land her father inhabited. Lord William turned his head, looked over his shoulder, and caught her gaze. His mouth stretched in a lazy smile.

She clenched her hands, but would not be seen to back away. Her face a mask, Lanora followed her aunt, who marched directly to Lord William. The circle of women gave way as he turned, stepped forward, and bowed.

"Lady Edith." He had a rich, deep voice. Experience told Lanora she could recognize it across a room. "I do not know if you recall, but we were introduced some time ago. I'm--"

"Lord William." Her aunt's tone was impartial. "You have the look of your father about you."

Did Lanora imagine the shadow that darkened his eyes?

"You will hold that against me, I take it?" His tone was light, but the shadow remained.

Aunt Edith shook her head. "No, for you're more your mother's son, I think, and she was a good soul."

The surrounding women murmured, exchanging looks. Everyone must suspect Aunt Edith meant to insult the future marquess, accusing him of being like his mad, violent mother. Knowing her aunt, Lanora thought not.

Lord William certainly seemed offended, though, all light leaving his eyes. Smile frozen in place, he looked past Aunt Edith and bowed to Lanora. "I'm afraid I have not had the pleasure of being introduced to your niece."

CHAPTER SEVEN

William took Lady Lanora's extended hand, bowing over it. Thus far, he'd maintained his distance, for she and her father could easily learn he'd never set foot in Egypt. Now, he found the cold perfection glimpsed from afar was nothing compared to the spark held deep in her emerald green eyes.

"Lord William." She annunciated with precision, but he'd heard her speaking as Mrs. Smith. He could tease from those short syllables the soft country lilt she kept hidden.

"Lady Lanora. I have long wished to avail myself of your renowned beauty for the length of a set."

The aunt, frumpy and too-shrewd, gave a satisfied nod and turned away, effectively cutting them off from the gaggle of matrons at his back.

"Is that your version of requesting a dance, my lord?"

William couldn't contain a smile as he permitted his gaze to roam over her. She was so very cool. Her façade was impeccable. If he didn't know she donned dowdy garb and passed out bread in the poorest corner of London, he would have deemed her not worth his while. Her beauty was flawless, but William required something more than outward charms to stir his interest. At the least, a woman should have a notion of how they might enjoy themselves.

Not a line marred Lady Lanora's brow as she attempted to tug her fingers from his. "I can see you are confounded by a simple question. If you'll excuse me, my lord."

Far from relinquishing her, William raised her hand to brush a kiss across her knuckles. "My apologies. I was struck dumb by your beauty. That was, indeed, my attempt at inviting you to dance."

With an assertive pull, she drew her hand away. "I'm afraid, though my card is not yet filled out, my time is promised. I have existing arrangements."

"Oh? With someone special?" Which would ruin his plans. If he must be courting someone from Lethbridge's list, Lady Lanora was the only remotely interesting option.

She cast a quick look about at the growing ring of observers. "No one is special, my lord."

Did she truly mean no one was special, or was she simply trying to disparage the hungry looking fellows who edged nearer to overhear them? Fortune hunters. Bounders. Social climbers. She was correct. Not a one of them was worthy of her.

"Surely you have a waltz free?" He hadn't thought her frame could go any more rigid, but it did.

"Only because, as you have must have observed, I do not approve of the dance."

So rumor had it. "I've never seen you attempt it, whether to approve or disapprove." He added a touch of mockery to his tone.

"Why should I attempt that which is scandalous?"

He leaned near, lowering his voice. "If you agree to one waltz with me, I shall not make a scene here and now."

"Extortion, my lord?" Her eyes narrowed. "I should have thought, even with your reputation, such tactics would be beneath you."

William offered a lazy smile, one that served him well with all manner of women. "So you follow my reputation? Then you should know I am the worst sort of scoundrel. No tactic is beneath me when confronted with beauty such as yours."

"You seek to impress me with your infamy?"

If not for the quickening of her pulse, discernable in her slender neck, he would have deemed her wholly unaffected. "Women love a bounder." He held up a hand before she could speak. "You will deny it, but they do. Look to every parlor in London. You'll find clippings of that rogue Lefthook, carefully gathered by trembling hands and oft clutched to heaving maidenly bosoms."

"From what I have heard, Lord Lefthook is not a rogue at all." Her words were clipped. "Though obviously a man of little means, he risks himself to aid others."

"A man of little means, is he?" The idea amused William.

"It can be deduced he knows the part of the city he roams rather well, as he's not known to have failed in any of his feats. He apparently patrols it with ease." She shrugged, the motion much more entrancing than when most women employed it. "Therefore, he lives there. How else could he be so familiar?"

"And a man who lives in that borough must be poor." Like all the *ton*, she would look down on one who didn't reside in the proper part of London.

Green eyes studied him. William realized he'd let a hint of bitterness touch his voice. He endeavored for another easy smile. It felt stale.

"A poor man can be every inch as good as a wealthy man," her words were soft. "An argument might be made that it's more likely so."

William didn't conceal his surprise. This was the hidden side of Lady Lanora. "Hardly a fitting philosophy for the daughter of a duke."

The coldness in her demeanor redoubled. "I daresay not. My point remains. Lefthook is obviously an honorable man." She squared her shoulders. "Unlike you, my lord."

He raised his eyebrows, taken aback in spite of her reputation for putting men in their places. "If you were a man, I would challenge you for that."

"If I were a man, I would meet you at dawn," she said without a hint of prevarication.

How marvelous she was. He hadn't dreamed the ice queen of the *ton* contained such fire. "I can think of a much more enjoyable way for us to be together come dawn."

He braced himself for a slap and the shock that would race through the room, confirming both their reputations. Instead, she looked down. Though the action concealed much, he could see her cheeks round. Was Lady Lanora smiling at his innuendo?

Her lack of composure gave him the moments he required to regain his. "Agree to one waltz with me, my lady," he pressed, now eager to experience the feel of her in his arms. "I can promise you the reason it's scandalous is because it's quite enjoyable."

She looked up, her face smooth of expression, but her gaze contemplative. She possessed the most striking eyes he'd ever seen.

"The truth is, I do not know how to waltz."

His eyebrows shot up again.

"If you tell anyone, I shall put it out that you asked me to marry you," she added.

He grinned. "Threats, my lady? I would have thought such tactics beneath you."

She made an airy gesture with one long-fingered hand. "I have an absent father. It's likely I've not been raised well. We have spoken long enough, my lord. We're garnering attention."

As he wished, for word would get back to the marquess that William was following orders. Still, it wouldn't do to put his quarry too much on guard.

"Of course. My apologies. I'm sure you do not wish to have your name sullied by association."

"One would think as much, wouldn't one?" She curtsied.

William bowed, oddly stung she hadn't disagreed. He turned and strode away. Men flocked about her in his wake, setting his teeth on edge.

He didn't remain at the ball, but headed outside to call for his carriage. After two encounters with Lady Lanora, though she knew of only one, William was rather certain he had a problem. That problem, as usual, was the marquess. The old man said William must marry. Lady Lanora was on Lethbridge's list. William knew, though, that she wouldn't be if the marquess had reviewed it.

Lady Lanora was more apt than any other person in London to discover that William had never been to Egypt, let alone lived there until he reappeared at age fourteen. She might feel sympathy for London's poor. She might wax compassionately on the worth of a man, but he knew his peers. If she learned he'd grown up in the slums of London, she would disdain him. Worse, she would reveal his secret to the *ton*.

The trouble was, now that he'd met her, William was intrigued. Her raven locks and sparkling emerald eyes set her apart from other ladies of the *ton*. Her lithe form, gently curved in the most desirable places, begged a man to put his hands on her, and he was resolved to. William would have his waltz.

More than that, beneath a façade obviously designed to keep the world at a distance, resided a keenness of wit in her eyes, and a spark. It made sense, being the daughter of a renowned scholar and explorer. As Darington's daughter was. William could tell from the man's letters she was intelligent. Was Lady Lanora similarly so? He feared she might be.

Equally disturbing was the stab of fury as he walked away, while other men crowded her. No woman had inspired that spark of possessiveness in him. He was very worried it was the seed of attraction. With that seed planted, it would be impossible to consider any of the other suggested women. If William must bind himself to one of the *ton's* diamonds, it would be one for whom he felt at least a spark of desire.

When his carriage arrived, William told his man to take him to the marquess's London home. They set out for the Westlock residence, where William had spent the first four years of his life, and then four more, before heading to the reprieve of university. After that, he'd established his own household. He'd sworn never to reside under the same roof with the old man again.

The marquess would think rebelliousness drove William to select Lady Lanora from Lethbridge's list. Let him. That was safer than giving the old man any truth, for knowledge was leverage, and giving the marquess leverage was dangerous. If he wanted William married, he would have to agree with William's choice. It was Lady Lanora or no one. She was the first woman of the *ton* to stir so much as a flicker of interest in him.

His resolve marshalled, when the carriage stopped at the marquess's home, William vaulted from the vehicle. The house was a stern, sever building, and dark. Almost a blight on the wealthy London street, though faultlessly maintained. The marquess's butler, a man whose face didn't move even when he spoke, opened the door. He bowed, accepting William's hat and gloves.

"He's in his office?" William asked.

"Yes, my lord."

Halfway down the hall, grim ancient faces glared at him from gilt frames on the flock-clad walls, William reined in his purposeful strides and slowed. He took several deep breaths. A confrontation of wills was best avoided. The marquess held too many cards. Lighter steps brought him to the dark mahogany door. He knocked, pressed the door open before the sound died, and stepped in. He took petty delight in the minor disrespect.

As always, the sturdy form of the marquess filled the large leather-upholstered chair behind the desk. William closed the door, attention on the old man as he passed matching leather couches and continued to the chair before the desk. The marquess didn't stand. William didn't bow.

The marquess set aside his pen, dropping a blotting page over his work. "You've come about your marriage."

It was difficult to tell in the flickering lamplight, but the old man looked drawn. William liked to imagine there was an unhealthy yellow tinge to his skin. "You would force me to wed in twenty days."

"Under twenty now. Your score of days began when you signed. In spite of your numerous weaknesses, I expect you know how to count. I also expect you to honor your word." The marquess coughed. He took out a handkerchief and wiped his mouth, then shoved the square back in his pocket.

How William longed to wrest the handkerchief from him, in the hope it held blood. "And I expect you to honor yours, old man. If I wed a woman from that list, the Westlock fortunes are mine."

"Lethbridge assured me they are all quality breeding stock. If you get one to bind herself to you, you'll deserve the wealth that goes along with our name."

"Then I select Lady Lanora Hadler."

The marquess eyed him for a long moment. He slammed a palm down on the desk. William didn't flinch, though the sound ricocheted through the wood paneled room. "Lethbridge."

"Yes, Lethbridge. That's what you get for leaving something as important as the Westlock line to a lackey."

The marquess coughed again, for longer this time. The handkerchief came out, was applied, and disappeared. William watched with avid interest.

"Yes, I'm dying," the marquess growled. "I'm sure you'll have quite the celebration when I'm gone."

"Only as is right to honor your exulted life, my lord."

"Spare me your insolence. You will not court Solworth's daughter. You know the risk."

"If I wed her before she learns I never lived in Egypt, my secret will be doubly safe. She'll be bound to me. She won't dare reveal the truth then."

The marquess drummed his fingers on the desk. He shook his head. "The risk is too great, greater than you realize. Besides, how will you marry the chit? She has what, eighteen years? You don't have the time to write her father for permission and receive a reply."

William forced a smile. Damn the old bastard for being right. William hadn't considered that. "I'll think of something, never fear. Perhaps a trip to Scotland is in order."

The marquess grunted. "I've heard of the girl. They say she's as warm as a corpse. You'll have little luck there. If you wish to set yourself an impossible task, so be it."

"You think she'll prove impervious to my charms?"

"She's Solworth's daughter. She'll prove too intelligent to bed you."

William leaned forward. He took in the deep shadows draped under the marquess's bloodshot eyes. "A wager? If I can get it in writing, within my twenty days, that she'll wed me, you set aside this notion of signing the new will. Throw it on the fire."

The marquess shook his head. "Women have no honor. What's to say she won't sign and then back out? No, I want one wedded and bedded before I die." He fell into another fit of coughing.

"Fine, wedded it is, by Gretna Green, if I must. I put my name to that page and I will honor it, but you will honor the names listed."

"Do as you will," the marquess wheezed. "Pursue all the women on the list if you like. Manage to wed one of them, even Solworth's chit, and the Westlock fortune is yours."

"You're too kind, my lord." William stood. "If you'll excuse me."

The brief interview was all the time he could remain in the marquess's presence before images of his mother, dying, and locked in a cell would fill his vision until it turned red with rage. There had been times before he went to university when only fear kept him from pounding the life from the man. In the years since, that fear had disappeared, leaving behind coiled anger.

The marquess answered with another grunt. He moved the ink blotter and retrieved his pen. William closed the door firmly on his way out.

CHAPTER EIGHT

Lanora was inexplicably miffed when Lord William never returned to claim his waltz. Not that she'd agreed to one, but she expected him to insist. His hazel eyes were a stormy blue-green as they talked, giving her the impression his interest was more than passing. But, that was the way of a rogue, making a woman feel he meant more than he said. Still, each time a waltz began, a breathless anticipation touched her, but she never saw his tall form again.

Until she went to sleep. Then they waltzed endlessly through her dreams. They also spoke of Mr. Darington and her father, though Lanora couldn't remember what was said. In her dreams, she took Lord William to see the home for women Mr. Darington was building, only to find an empty square of land.

She woke early and gave up on the pretense of rest. She didn't know what her mind was trying to tell her, with the mix of dancing and talking. Obviously, Lord William was handsome. More so than the average gentleman, being taller, with a physique that bespoke strength, but that shouldn't warrant a restless night. Perhaps it was her failure to inquire about Mr. Darington? Lord William represented an opportunity to pass along her concern about the lack of progress on the home for women. Lanora, too caught up in his charms, had squandered that chance.

She slipped from bed and began to ready for the day, her brows puckered in a frown. She'd spent the previous evening thinking about Lord William. Then the entire night. Now, he filled her morning thoughts. If she didn't know better, she'd worry she was developing some sort of infatuation with the man.

That, of course, was impossible. Impeccable tailoring and good looks aside, he was a rake. He was one step above a highwayman. She'd rather have an absurd infatuation with the unknown Lord Lefthook, like all the other ladies of London.

Still, she found she couldn't put Lord William from her mind, especially the strain in his voice when he spoke of the poorest part of London. It was an odd tone for a future marquess. Then there was her aunt's tacit approval of him.

Perhaps that was the trouble. Her aunt's words in the carriage had wheedled their way into Lanora's mind. Aunt Edith knew precisely where to strike; the people who would someday be beholden to Lanora. She loved her home and the people there. She would never leave them to the uncertainty of who-knew-what remote relation, or have the land reverted to the crown to be overseen from afar. The only way to stop that was to have a child, and the only way for that to happen was to marry.

Give up her freedom. Have someone there to tell her Grace was her maid, not her friend. That she couldn't celebrate Christmas with the staff, or attend country dances. Could she give up her life to ensure the future of those she cared for? What if she bore a son and he grew up to be a rake, like his father?

Lanora gave her head a vigorous shake. Why would her son's father be a rake? She would not marry a rake, especially not Lord William. She'd spoken with the man once. He hadn't even returned to dance with her. Likely, he'd already forgotten their exchange. She was being ridiculous.

Lanora made her way to the breakfast parlor, a silly affectation. At home, she ate in the kitchen with the staff. Why force Cook and her helpers to rise early, devote the morning to creating a cornucopia of items, then carry them all into a parlor, employing a ludicrous number of platters and plates, so that Lanora could pick out the two items she wanted and eat alone at a giant table?

Here, though, that was how it must be. Her aunt seemed to enjoy the breakfast parlor, and the selection, as did her terriers. Much of Cook's work went into dogs' bellies. Grace also assured Lanora that word would get out if she behaved in so odd a manner, for staff gossiped. On top of that, much of the food was repurposed to serve with tea in the event of callers, and everything that was left was consumed by the staff, who would be dismayed not to receive it. So, with the entire household arrayed against her, Lanora must dine alone in the breakfast parlor, while her aunt and the pups snored the morning away in their rooms and Grace ate in the kitchen in the company of friends.

Lanora nibbled on toast and sipped her tea, the *Times* open before her. Another joy a husband would undoubtedly take from her. He would claim the paper first, likely not deeming her mind capable of understanding it.

"Why are you making that face?" Grace said as she entered the room. She carried her gloves and hat. "Who has angered you?"

Lanora set her teacup down. "No one." She shrugged. "Rather, men. My aunt says I must have one."

"You know she's correct." Grace's look was sympathetic.

"You don't have one. She doesn't have one. Cook doesn't have one."

"None of us have your responsibilities." Grace smiled. "Besides, how can I become your cook if you stay in your father's country house and dine in the kitchen? You're to have a home of your own, and proper meals, and entertain."

She took in Grace's dreamy tone and sighed. "Yes, well, at least one of us shall be happy."

"We will find you a gentleman who makes you happy. We'll simply investigate them, like we do at home before dispensing charity."

"There's no village to ask around, and we can hardly walk over and survey each man's holdings, as we would a farm."

"This is London." Grace's smile turned sly. "It's easier. We simply bribe a man's servants and we shall know all. When I return from the paper, you shall tell me if there are any gentlemen in particular who make you go all calf-eyed, and we'll send out footmen to bribe their staff."

"Wonderful." Lanora didn't hide her lack of enthusiasm.

"It will be, as will bargaining the best price for this Lefthook story." Grace donned her hat and tied the ribbon under her chin.

"You're not to give your name, or Mrs. Banke's."

"I know. I won't be long." She pulled on her gloves and, with a jaunty wave, left the parlor.

Lanora sighed, envious of Grace's freedom. Lady Lanora Hadler could never go to the paper with a story about Lord Lefthook. She would become the story. Grace could go. She could give a false name, or none at all, and no one would press her. They wouldn't care who she was in view of what she had to tell.

Grace could be a cook and eat in the kitchen if she liked, and not marry if she didn't find a man she wished to wed. Lanora knew many lady's maids didn't live as happily as Grace. They were put upon, demeaned, made to endure uncertainty and, sometimes, unwanted attention from the men of the house. Still, in that moment, being Grace seemed more preferable than being the only child of a duke.

Irritated with her petulance, Lanora gave up on her toast and went to the library to browse her grandfather's collection. She preferred her father's books in their country home. Still, searching through those assembled by her more distant ancestors, who preferred London, was interesting. She liked to imagine her father there as a child, and tried to pick out the books he would have been drawn to. That strategy soon found her in the front parlor, where the light was best, reading the *Iliad* in archaic Greek.

Much of it was tricky, for the Greek she'd learned was modern, but that made it all the more entertaining. After all, she already knew the story. She'd read it several times, in several languages. She sat curled in an armchair near the window, engrossed, when someone cleared their throat.

Lanora looked up to find a wild-eyed maid standing in the parlor doorway. Behind her loomed the darkly clad form of Lord William. She stared, feeling as bereft as the maid obviously was. No one visited their home, not after her cold treatment of the first handful of guests, and certainly not men. Definitely not rakes.

"I came to see if you're in, my lady." The maid rolled her eyes and grimaced. Obviously, she wanted Lanora to know she'd tried to dissuade Lord William from following her to the parlor.

Lanora brought her feet to the floor and stood. "Apparently I am." Over the girl's head, she took in Lord William's lazy smile. "Could you see if my aunt is about? I'm sure she'd like to greet Lord William."

"Yes, my lady." The girl curtsied and hurried away.

He entered, shrinking the room with his presence. Lanora inclined her head in response to his bow. Marking her place, she set the *Iliad* in her chair and moved to the sofa before the low table where refreshments would be served, if he accepted any.

"Would you care to sit, my lord? Shall I call for refreshments?"

"No, thank you. I've recently dined." Two long strides took him to the chair. He scooped up her book. His eyebrows swooped upward as he paged through it. "You read Greek? This Greek?"

Of course, he didn't think her, a mere woman, capable of reading the manuscript. She shrugged. She didn't miss the way his gaze dropped from her face to take in the motion. "It passes the time. Do sit, please."

He snapped the book closed, a sly glint in his eyes. "I'm not here to socialize."

"That seems highly unreasonable, my lord, as this is the hour for socializing, and you have come to my parlor."

"I am here to teach you to waltz."

Lanora swallowed, her treacherous pulse quickening at the thought of his arms about her. "That is not necessary, my lord."

"But it is. You've too fine a form not to be waltzed about every ballroom in London. Think of the grace you're depriving us all of."

"I agree," Aunt Edith said. She entered the room amidst a sea of terriers.

Lanora relaxed at the sight of them. In her experience, city folk baulked when confronted with a swarm of scruffy country dogs. Some of the ladies who'd visited when Lanora and Aunt Edith first arrived in town had even screamed. Lanora smiled at the memory.

Her anticipation turned to surprise as Lord William tossed the book to the table and dropped to a knee in the middle of the parlor. He pulled off his gloves then rubbed unkempt ears and patted shaggy heads. Stubby terrier tails thumped. There wasn't a single growl. The pups were entranced. Only Aunt Edith's Skye Terrier, always reserved, remained at her side.

"I heard you've prize stock, Lady Edith," he said. "They don't disappoint. Irish, Scottish, Welsh and, of course, some fine English lads."

Wonderful. He liked terriers, and they apparently adored him. Her aunt would take that as a sign.

"And lasses." Aunt Edith smiled benignly down at her pups. "You are correct, Lord William, Lanora should learn to waltz. I hear it's all the thing with you young folks. I believe she's been teaching several of the girls to play. I'm sure one of them can manage a waltz. Come, the pianoforte is in the large parlor."

"Splendid," Lord William said, a hint of surprised flickered across his face. With a few more pats for the pups, he stood, then grinned down at her.

"Fine," Lanora snapped. She frowned at his smile. He thought by winning over her aunt and the pups he could win her, did he? But…why? What on earth possessed a man like Lord William to wish to win her over?

He gestured for Lanora to precede him as Aunt Edith led the way to the large parlor. Not bothering with London manners, Aunt Edith raised her voice as they walked and called for the maid who was most accomplished on the piano. Lanora squared her shoulders, refusing to be embarrassed by her aunt's behavior.

The maid came scurrying as they entered the parlor.

"Ah, there's a dear girl," Aunt Edith said. She settled into a highbacked chair. The ancient fabric of her riding habit rustled as her terriers arrayed themselves at her feet, several laying on her hem. "Be a good girl and play a waltz. Lord William is here to teach Lanora to dance."

"Yes, my lady." The girl curtsied, hardly able to drag her eyes from Lord William as she crossed to the piano.

He looked about the cream and blue parlor, his gaze skimming across the furniture. "May I reposition the chairs?"

"As you see fit," Aunt Edith said.

"I can call a footman," Lanora offered, watching him approach a sturdy armchair.

The look he cast her was amused. "That won't be necessary."

Lanora couldn't help but watch as he easily lifted the chair and carried it to the side of the room. Several more followed. His shoulders bunched under his well-fitted coat, but he showed no strain. He cut an impressive figure, but then a rake must, for his charms were his weapon.

He turned back to her, the emerald color of his vest glinting under his coat, and held out a hand. "My lady."

Lanora pressed her lips closed. There was no winning an argument against her aunt, the terriers and Lord William. She crossed to him, then she took his hand, belatedly realizing neither of them wore gloves. The warmth of his palm, skin slightly rougher than her own, sent a heat through her that threatened to reach her face.

"I'm afraid I'm not dressed for dancing," she said, relieved her tone held steady.

"Nor am I. We must make do."

Did he have to speak in that low, rumbling tone, his gaze locked on hers as if they shared some secret? He took her other hand, raising it to his shoulder. He dropped his hand to her waist. Her heart beat at an unacceptable rate, making her lightheaded.

"You begin with your right leg," he continued. "I shall step forward with my left and you shall retreat."

He pressed his leg to hers. Lanora stepped back quickly. His hands braced her.

"Now across, then together," he said, moving them through the steps. "The basic step is despairingly simple. The key is to move in harmony. This is aided by music." He looked toward the pianoforte.

With a start, the maid turned from them. She began to play.

Lord William returned his attention to Lanora, his smile warm. "Now, on my count, we'll begin."

Lanora was stiff at first, more because of how disconcerting it was to have him clasping her hand, his other pressed firmly to her waist, than because of the dance steps. She hadn't properly realized how thin the material of her cream-colored day dress was. She could feel the heat of him through the fabric.

She attempted to concentrate on the steps, but his nearness flooded her senses. The scent of shaving soap and clean linen. The intensity of his blue-green eyes. His crooked smile under artfully disarrayed curls. How could she learn a dance in such conditions?

"I read that the gentleman must look over the lady's shoulder except during a turn," she said. She suppressed a grimace at her breathless tone.

"You mean, if I'm to look at you, we must turn?" He swung her about, her feet skimming the floor as a strong arm pulled her against his body to make the turn.

Lanora's face heated. She firmed her arms, opening space between them. "I most certainly do not mean that, and I do not believe that's how I've seen other couples dance."

His smile widened. "So we are a couple?"

"What is it you want from me?" she whispered. He couldn't possibly imagine she would dally with him, nor could he have honorable intentions toward her. His presence in her home was baffling.

"I want you to agree to a ride in the park tomorrow."

"My lord, I can't imagine—"

"Where we may speak with more discretion."

His eyes darkened with entreaty. Lanora was dismayed by how moved she was to accept. Lord William's reputation was well earned. He was a dangerous man. That still didn't explain what he required of her, a duke's daughter and a virgin.

"Agreeing to a ride will put an end to today's meeting?"

He winced slightly, but nodded. "My company is so terrible?"

"Your company is confusing and unwarranted."

"I shall not agree to the second, for you are indeed waltzing."

Lanora blinked. In her distraction, she'd fallen into easy step with him. They flowed across the room, as if they'd waltzed together many times, as if she knew the dance well.

The music stopped. He stepped away, bowing over her hand. "It has been my pleasure, my lady."

Lanora curtsied. "Thank you for the instruction, my lord."

Lord William turned to her aunt with another bow. "Lady Edith."

"Lord William." Her aunt offered a nod. "My old eyes appreciated the display. Lanora improved markedly under your tutelage."

"It was her natural grace, my lady, and little to do with me." With a final bow, he strode from the room.

Several of the pups rose to follow him. Lanora stood, rooted to the spot. She frowned, then hurried out. She must know more. This was absurd. Why was Lord William giving the impression of a man courting her? She, who all knew didn't wish to be courted, being pursued by a man all knew didn't wish to wed. Ridiculous.

Remembering Grace's earlier mention of spying on gentlemen, Lanora used the servants' stairs to retrieve a purse of coins from her room. Quick steps brought her to the footman just returning from opening the door to Lord William's carriage.

"Joseph, did you hear where he instructed his driver to go?" she asked.

"Yes, my lady."

Lanora held out the purse. "Follow him. Discreetly, of course. I want to know everywhere he goes today."

Joseph bowed. "Yes, my lady."

LATER THAT DAY, WHEN GRACE returned with Mrs. Banke's coin, Lanora listened to her tale of bargaining at the *Times* and then imparted the details of Lord William's visit. That evening, they both sat up in the parlor, waiting for Joseph's report on Lord William's doings. It was late when he finally came in, but not so late as Lanora expected.

"My lady. Grace," he greeted.

"I hope your day was not too long, Joseph?" Lanora said. "Please sit."

A London servant, Joseph failed to hide his shock at the offer. "No thank you, my lady. I prefer to stand."

Lanora doubted that, but didn't press him. "What have you to report?"

"Lord William went to Whites and another, less savory club. Gambling, I believe."

She nodded. That was to be expected.

"He took a ride in the park. Fine horseflesh he has, handles it well, too, my lady."

"Well, that's good news," Grace said, looking pleased.

"As if riding well makes a man a worthy husband." Lanora rolled her eyes toward the intricate plaster molding on the ceiling.

"You'll want to live in the country." Grace folded her hands in her lap, her words crisp. "You want a man who can ride."

"Do not marry me to the rogue yet, Grace. Continue, please, Joseph."

"I returned because Lord William went to, ah, visit a friend, and I don't think he'll be out anytime soon."

"A friend?" Lanora asked sharply, alerted by Joseph's tone.

Joseph rattled off an address, dropping his gaze.

Lanora went cold. "I see." The street was so notorious for housing the mistresses of the wealthy, it was colloquially called Mistress's Row. "And you believe he will remain for some time?"

"I watched for a spell, my lady. He was still inside when I left."

Lanora nodded.

"It doesn't have to mean what you think," Grace said, her tone tentative.

"Doesn't it?" Lanora shook her head, surprised by the strength of her disappointment. "Was that all, then, Joseph?"

"There was one other thing, my lady. I followed Lord William all day after he left here." Joseph's face was perplexed. "Thing is, some other bloke was following him too. I stayed out of his sight. He was still watching that house when I left."

Lenora hesitated. That was strange. "Thank you, Joseph. You've done well. I'm sorry to ask you to make such a long day of it."

"It's no trouble, my lady. We all want you to marry well."

Lanora forced a smile. "Thank you."

Joseph bowed, then left the parlor.

Grace turned to Lanora. "Who do you suppose was following your Lord William?"

"You know he is not, nor ever will be, my Lord William. Really, Grace, of all the men to pin your hopes on."

"He did come to teach you to waltz and asked you to ride in the park. That's romantic." Grace let out a dreamy sigh.

Lanora shook her head. "As to who else followed him, I'm sure it was the footman of some other poor, besieged lady, or a jealous lover, or an even more jealous husband. Nothing we want to involve ourselves in, certainly."

Grace's sigh was more forlorn this time. "I suppose you're correct. Still, coming here to dance with you was romantic, and I know you, Lanora. You aren't as disinterested in him as you wish me to believe."

Lanora pressed her lips together, considering her answer. Grace did know her, and she was correct. "He's very charming. Too much so. It's difficult to ascertain if any emotion one feels toward him is real, or if anything he says is."

"Then there's nothing for it. Before this gets out of hand, you shall have to kiss him."

"I beg your pardon?" Lanora stared at Grace, shocked.

"It's the only way to know for sure. If you kiss him, you will know if you care for him and if he cares for you. I'm certain of it. Then you can plan accordingly. A man can always be separated from his mistress, after all."

"You're daft."

"It's true. He can be weaned from her, as well as from his gambling. Men are malleable creatures. How do you think women manage? Men have all the power, yes, but we slowly mold them to our will. It's for our own survival."

"Grace, that's so…mercenary."

"I didn't shape the world, Lanora." Grace's expression softened. "For all your learning, you're terribly naive about some things."

"Well, naive or not, I will hold out for a gentleman I actually care for, just the way he is. Your way sounds like an awful lot of trouble, and has the chance of failure." It also sounded rather unfeeling.

"All the more reason to kiss him. Only once, mind you. Don't permit it to get out of hand, and don't forget you've hairpins for a reason."

Lanora shook her head. "I will not kiss Lord William."

"So you say now, but I know you would rather have questions answered than not."

"If someone saw, I would be made to wed him." Grace's vague promise of an answer seemed hardly worth the risk of being forced to marry him should they be caught.

"He's a rake. He will arrange for you to be unobserved."

Lanora shook her head. She turned the topic to other things. Soon, they retired for the night. Try as she might, though, as she lay in bed seeking sleep, she could not dispel from her mind the idea of kissing Lord William.

CHAPTER NINE

William contained the urge to whistle as he maneuvered the light, open carriage down Lady Lanora's street. The day was fine, sky blue, sun bright. It was a day made for charming a lady in the park.

Lady Lanora was too intelligent to simply be charmed, however. He hadn't missed the suspicion in her, in spite of the effect he knew he had. And that book. Anyone who could read that jumble of archaic Greek had quite the head on their shoulders.

He might, as a last resort, need to offer her some truths. Not all, by any means. Knowledge gave a person power, and he wasn't ready to let anyone have that much power over him. Even Cecilia didn't know he'd never been to Egypt. Only the marquess knew all, and often wielded the knowledge. He held William under the constant threat of defamation, and now he'd added losing the Greydrake fortune to his arsenal. William grimaced, wishing reputation and coin held less sway in his life.

Fortunately, arrival at the Solworth London home revived his spirits. Lady Lanora appeared, slipping out a narrowly open door. She pushed several terriers back inside with a slipper-clad foot, offering an enticing glimpse of a slender ankle. Her gown was pale yellow, similar to all young ladies' gowns, save for the splendidness of her figure. Her shiny black locks were neatly arranged, her green eyes once again as cold as the gems they resembled.

"My lady," he greeted as a footman helped her into the carriage.

"Lord William."

Her tone was excessively cool. She didn't look at him. Surely, she wasn't that angry over a single waltz with her aunt and a maid in the room?

William maneuvered the carriage back into the light street traffic. By the time they reached the park, he'd become uncomfortable with her determined silence. Her smile was so tight as to appear pained. Anyone looking on them, and there were many about, would think he held a pistol to her side to make her remain in the carriage with him.

Out of respect for the woman he thought her to be, he decided to take a direct approach. "You do not seem happy to ride with me."

Her eyes darted toward him and away. "I cannot fathom your intention in taking this drive."

"You cannot? Is it not obvious I'm courting you?"

Her eyes widened slightly. Her jaw clenched. She cast a look about, at the numerous other occupants of the park. "You jest."

"I do not."

A line marred her brow. She turned to him with a frown. "Why would you court me? Have you a wager going?"

He kept an affable expression, though taken aback by her accusation. He'd known convincing her would be difficult. "There is no wager. I wish us to wed."

She blinked several times. "You hardly know me. Did my aunt put you up to this?"

"Your aunt?" He shook his head. He'd hoped for a slightly more enthusiastic response. "Lady Edith has nothing to do with my courting you. As for knowing you, I have watched you from afar. I'm quite smitten, I assure you."

"Smitten?" She gave him a cold smile. "I think perhaps your definition of the word differs from mine. Were I smitten with someone, I wouldn't spend the evening with my mistress."

This time, William couldn't hide his surprise. He recovered quickly, knowing many eyes were on them. "You had me followed."

She shrugged. "Of course. I wished to gauge your sincerity."

"And you found it lacking."

"Obviously."

She might believe she'd put him in his place, but William was pleased. A woman with no interest would never have him followed. It said much that she'd gone to the trouble. He was glad to learn his effect on her was more than physical.

"I can explain."

"I'm certain you can offer all manner of excuses, but I've no desire to hear them."

He grinned. She could be so cold, her tone infinitely condescending. It was an art. Lady Lanora was a work of art, from her flawless features to her well-modulated voice. He wondered if she could manage other facades as readily as she did *ton* diamond-an- devout widow.

"You find my lack of interest entertaining, my lord?"

No. He found the banked anger in her green eyes irresistible. What would that heat be like, unleashed? He knew better than to ask. "You will not hear me out? I thought you a lady of intelligence."

"That is an artless tactic, my lord."

"I am an artless sort of fellow."

"I doubt that."

"Lady Lanora." He lowered his voice to a husky murmur, leaning toward her. It wasn't fair, but he made no claim to be. "Please. Permit me one opportunity to explain myself. Is that so much to ask?"

She swallowed. Her pulse raced in her slender neck. "Very well."

"Excellent." He flipped the reins, angling them toward a flower garden constructed of blooms and walls of carefully trimmed evergreen. He knew well the garden's discreet paths. When they reached it, he brought the carriage to a halt and jumped down. One of the street boys lingering there ran up. William gave him a coin to watch the carriage before walking round to Lady Lanora's side. She was looking straight ahead, her posture rigid.

"It will be easier to speak if we're of a level." He held up a hand to her.

She cast him a quick glance, as if looking at him would ruin her resolve. "Why have we stopped?"

"What I wish to tell you is of a very sensitive nature. I seek privacy."

She gave a little shake of her head. "Grace said you would attempt to get me alone," she murmured, as if speaking to herself.

"Who is Grace?" He cast about in his mind. He couldn't recall Lady Lanora having any friends, let alone one named Grace. Then, he didn't know the name of every Miss in London.

"My dearest friend. You would not know her. She came with me from the country."

"And did this Grace give you advice for when I made my fateful attempt?"

"She would wish me to allow it."

He grinned. "I like her already."

The look Lady Lanora gave him was oddly reproachful. "So you say now."

Feeling he was on uneven footing, knowing so little about her friend, William returned to his goal. "Will you walk with me in the flower garden, Lady Lanora? I promise not to attempt a waltz."

She sat for a long moment before nodding. Turning, she offered her hand. He clasped her fingers, helped her down and tucked her hand into his arm. To his surprise, she made no effort to break free, permitting him to remain at her side as they headed down the first gravel path. The crunching of his boots on stone filled the silence between them.

"You're lucky you may wear boots. Slippers are a dreadful bit of silliness," she said, surprising him again by breaking the silence.

"Are they?" He'd never given them much thought, aside from when he was slipping one from a delicate foot.

"They're dreadfully impractical. A set for every gown. Material that does not withstand water or dirt. Like as not, one evening will ruin them." Her smile was wistful. "In the country, I wear boots."

"You would be like your aunt, I see."

"How I wish I could be."

Why did she sound so sorrowful? What young woman lamented not being a dowdy old widow with a pack of dogs? Fine as Lady Edith's collection was, a pack of terriers hardly replaced a husband and children.

He led her around several turns, wending his way toward one of the five focal points of the somewhat maze-like rooms created by walls of evergreen. Fewer flowers were in evidence than at other times of the year, for spring was behind them or not yet come, depending on how he wished to view the world. The particular space he brought her to, however, boasted a statue of Achilles. He thought it might appeal to her, given her choice in reading.

"I didn't realize this was here." Her tone was pleased. She left his side to examine the statue.

"Not many do. This is a less frequented area of the park. Most people come to be seen, after all."

Her back stiffened. She turned slowly, cool gaze assessing. "And we are here for you to explain your behavior."

"Would you care to sit?" He gestured toward one of three benches placed around the statue.

After a moment's hesitation, she nodded. She moved to Achilles' right, for the statue faced the opening, the only side with no place to sit and view it. William sat once she had, angling himself toward her. Sunlight shown bright around them. Somewhere, in the distance, children laughed. He opened his mouth, then closed it again. He spent so much time lying, he wasn't sure where to begin with the truth.

The one thing he was sure of was that he must not reveal he'd lived in London's poorest borough for the many years he was absent from the marquess's household. That would turn any well-bred lady from him, even a sympathetic one like Lady Lanora. Nor could he reveal who Cecilia truly was. Her safety was not a gambit. William shied from contemplation of what the marquess would do should he ever locate her.

"You were going to tell me why a smitten man visits his mistress," Lady Lanora said, her tone even.

She watched him with curious, slightly confused eyes. Did his expression reveal so much, then? Enough that she felt a softer touch was required. William grimaced. He may as well begin with something terrible, then. "My mother is dead, as you must know."

She nodded. "Yes, she and your older brother, both. I've heard the stories. After the…incident, she was brought to a place where she could be cared for, and you were sent to live with Mr. Darington, in Egypt, because your father was too heartbroken to look upon you."

The story the marquess told the world. William had used it to soften many a heart. How he wished he needn't begin his life with Lady Lanora on such lies. "That is… Well, yes, it's what they say, is it not?" He tried not to let subterfuge bog down his tongue. The truth was so much darker and more complicated. "Putting that aside, what is important here is that the marquess feels my mother was flawed. Weak."

That single line appeared on her brow again. She hadn't expected his words. "Weak?"

William nodded. "Unfit. Not worthy. Add most anything else disparaging you like and you'll have the gist."

"But I thought it was his sorrow that drove him to send you away." Her tone bled confusion.

As sorrow drove her father to leave when her mother died, he realized. Lady Lanora, who came from a home with a father who loved his wife and daughter, saw William's world in the same light. He passed a hand across his eyes, threading his way between truth and lie.

"The marquess is not a loving man."

Sympathy mounted in her expression.

William shook his head. He didn't wish to win her through pity. "Which is neither here nor there. What matters is, much of my life has been spent attempting to convince the marquess of my suitability. He requires an heir who is strong, lacks sentiment, knows his place in the realm, and a host of other archaic traits."

"You are telling me you've pretended to be a man different from who you are in order to please your father?" She sounded doubtful.

"It's simpler to obey the marquess than war with him, and yes, that is what I'm suggesting."

"And your mistress?"

"I have no mistress. I do keep a house, and a woman lives there, but she is not now, nor ever has she been, my lover. She is a ruse."

"And the gambling?"

He shook his head, his smile returning. "Many men gamble. I'm not saying I'm a saint, only that I didn't come courting you and then, hours later, avail myself of the charms of another."

She pressed her lips into a thin line. "It all sounds a bit farfetched."

"You have not met the marquess." God willing, she never would. William studied her, weighing his options. They were alone, utterly so. She was eighteen, on her first season. He'd read the effect his nearness had on her the first night they spoke, and while they danced. He was certain he could charm her, befuddle her, leave her mussed and dreamy eyed. That wasn't the way he wished to go about it, though, nor did he think it advisable.

Lady Lanora didn't strike him as the type to wed where her heart wasn't properly engaged, no matter what rash acts he drew her into. Worse, the way his blood surged at her nearness, the way the elusive sweet scent she wore reminded him of warm summer days, none of it boded well for his ability to stop once he began. That he could bring her around to agreement, at least for now, he did not doubt, but he would not deflower his future marchioness on a gravel walk under a statue of Achilles. Or lay her out on a stone bench and watch the sunlight caress her skin. Or—

"Lord William?"

He blinked, clearing visions of her from his mind.

"If you've no more compelling evidence to offer, I'm afraid I must insist you return me home."

William ran a slightly shaky hand through his hair. What was wrong with him, lusting after her like a schoolboy when he should be conversing intelligently? He must think of something more to say. He couldn't tell her anything else about Charles, or his mother. There must be something he could offer.

He mustered a crooked smile. "What more can I say? I'm not the man I show to society. I would be a good husband to you, not a cad who keeps mistresses and other bits on the side. Take the evidence before you. Have I attempted to seduce you? Have I been anything but a gentleman today?"

She studied him, her eyes guarded. "You are asking me to accept that your pursuit of me is in earnest, and you will be a model husband if we're to wed?"

"I am."

She pressed her lips together again, a habit he was beginning to believe meant she was struggling with an idea. "I will consider your words, but I must ask you to do something for me."

"If it's within my power." He spoke carefully, trying not to let the happiness that shot through him show. Showing more enthusiasm than a female evinced was apt to scare her off. Or so other men reported. William had never been in such a situation before meeting Lady Lanora. "What must I do?"

"I'm afraid you must kiss me."

Chapter Ten

Lanora worked not to wince. Lord William looked at her as if she'd suggested they flap their arms and fly up into the bright blue above, chasing clouds. What must he think of her? Here he was, a notorious rake and charmer, being perfectly well behaved, and she requested a kiss. If he refused, she was going to throttle Grace.

"It's a sad thing to find, at only six and twenty, that my hearing is failing me," he finally said.

"Are you declining, then?" She couldn't keep a hurt edge from her voice. She hadn't expected to be so thoroughly disappointed if he wouldn't kiss her. She'd expected relief.

"Before I decide, may I ask why?"

Lanora let out a sigh, feeling foolish. "Grace said, if I kissed you, I would better know my feelings, and she seems to think it will give me some insight into yours."

His eyebrows shot up. "And you agree with her?"

She shrugged. "I'm not certain. I worry you aren't the sort to stop with one kiss."

"Yet you would take that risk?" He didn't appear offended by the accusation. Nor did he refute it. If anything, amusement touched his tone.

"Well, if you don't stop, Grace said I was to remove a hairpin and stab you."

He grinned, a real smile, not the strained ones that curved his mouth as he spoke of his father. "What if kissing you is so distracting, I don't feel the hairpin?"

"Then I'll stab you again." She could feel her face heating.

His grin didn't falter. "Eventually, I should like to meet Grace."

Lanora doubted that would go well. She knew he believed Grace was at least a gentleman's daughter. When he learned she was a maid, he would look down on her, and Lanora. She frowned. How could she consider kissing such a man, any man of the *ton*?

"Or not," he said, his tone light. "As I can see you don't wish me to."

Her face was still hot. She stood, turning her back in the pretense of studying the sculpture. She could hear him rise to his feet. Once composed, she turned back. "Forgive me for making such a scandalous suggestion. Please forget I spoke."

His hazel eyes darkened. "I don't believe I can do that."

He was quite tall, particularly when he stood so near. Lanora pressed her lips together, annoyed by her racing pulse. "I rescind the request."

"Oh? Has it not worked in the past, then, kissing a man to know if there's something between you?" His tone was still light, but his eyes narrowed.

She lost a second battle not to blush. "I wouldn't know." Was that whispery voice hers?

"There's only one way to learn." He closed the remaining distance between them. "For the pursuit of knowledge, I feel you must permit me to kiss you."

He slid an arm around her waist, his hand warm and large on the small of her back. His other he brought to her face, his fingers gliding along a curl before tucking it behind her ear. His eyes, dark pools now, studied hers.

She should say no. She should step away. A proper lady wouldn't be in this empty garden with Lord William. A proper lady would already have a hairpin out.

Lanora closed her eyes and tilted her head back.

The moment his mouth touched hers, she forgot about hairpins, gardens, and proper ladies. His hand cupped her face, angling it. Resting her palms against his chest, she took in the warmth and strength of him. Nothing before had ever felt like his kiss. It was sunlight and joy. Her whole body came alive, when she hadn't known it wasn't. The kiss went on and on, enveloping, dizzying.

Then he stopped. Slowly, achingly, he raised his head. Lanora curled her fingers into the lapel of his coat. She rocked up on her toes, trying to reclaim the joy of moments before. He let out a low growl and wrapped both arms around her, crushing her to his chest. He rested his chin on her head. His warm breath stirred her hair. His heart pounded beneath her palm.

"What are you doing?" she whispered, laying her cheek against his coat.

"Stopping before you make me forget to."

"It was a good kiss, then?" She wished she could call the words back, they sounded so nervous.

His chuckle washed over her. She closed her eyes. The arms about her felt so safe. When was the last time she'd felt arms around her?

"I should take you home," he said. "We've been gone rather a while."

"Yes, of course." She stepped back, a little sad that he permitted her to. What did she think would happen? They would stand in the park kissing all afternoon? That was ridiculous.

"Here." He tugged at her gown, straightening it, and untucked her curl so it fell across her cheek once more. After scrutinizing her and making a few final adjustments, he fluffed his cravat, which she'd crushed.

The efficient, practiced way he managed it all, while she stood, her limbs still trembling, brought Lanora to her senses. The man before her was still Lord William Greydrake. He was a notorious rake. Likely, his words about courting her had already accomplished his goal. He'd won his kiss from one of the *ton's* most aloof ladies. If she proved lucky, he wouldn't boast about it. She'd probably never see him again.

He took her hand and placed it on his arm. As they retraced their path into the garden, Lanora pressed her lips together. She wasn't sure if she regretted what she'd done. She already felt drawn to kiss him again, and already doubted she ever would.

"What events do you attend tomorrow? May I claim my sets now, before your card fills?" he asked

She snapped her gaze to his, finding his eyes a light blue-green. A warm smile turned up his mouth. "Sets?" she parroted. He wished for more than one?

"Of course. I would have all London know I'm courting you."

She looked away, flummoxed. He really meant to court her? "We're attending the theater tomorrow evening."

"Then I shall as well, in hopes of glimpsing you."

"You truly mean to court me?"

"I admit, in view of my reputation, I can understand your doubt, but surely our kiss told you all?"

"It was…." Why had she developed such a propensity toward blushing? "I liked it very much."

His grin was smug.

As wonderful as his kiss was, Lanora still felt unease. She mulled on it. When they reached his carriage, she let him assist her up, but frowned. He tossed the boy another coin and climbed up, settling into the seat beside her. A flip of the reins set the well-trained horses moving.

"You hardly know me," she said. And she hardly knew him.

"I know you are intelligent and beautiful. I know you're more spirited than you would have the world believe."

"You aim to flatter."

He turned the team, taking them down a road that arced back to meet their earlier path. "I know your father works with Mr. Darington. I admit, that is much of what initially drew me to you. That we share Egypt, in an odd way."

His expression was guarded, his words almost halting. She didn't know what to make of such hesitancy in stating something they both knew, but it recalled the home for women. She berated herself for needing the reminder. How could she forget to ask about it a second time?

"You're in contact with Mr. Darington, I assume?"

"I am."

"Would you inquire after something for me when next you write him?"

He cast her a surprised look. "Certainly, but couldn't your father?"

It was her turn to look away, to feign indifference. "I've asked him, but my father is, well, distractible. He doesn't always read his letters, or always reply to them. I have no way to know if he read my words, or passed them on." She tried to keep the hurt of that admission from showing.

Lord William looked at her askance. "What is it you wish me to inquire of Darington?" he finally asked.

She was relieved he let the matter of her father's inattention pass. "As you likely know, he's funding a home for displaced women. I wish to make sure he knows work has stopped. I spoke to the foreman some days ago, and he said work would resume when the funds arrived."

"You spoke with the foreman?" He raised his eyebrows.

Lanora kept her gaze ahead. She must choose her words more carefully. "Or I asked one of my footmen to," she said, trying not to lie outright.

"You wish me to ensure Darington knows the funds he promised to build the house haven't been provided?"

She nodded, again thankful he was willing to let the conversation move forward. "I do. It's very important." She pressed her lips together, thinking. Lord William should understand her better before things got out of hand. Undoubtedly, their drive in the park already had them practically wed in the eyes of the *ton*. "You should know, I take a keen interest in improving the lives of people who have little."

"Duly noted."

Lanora frowned. "That is all you will say?" Was he taking her courtship seriously? "Your reputation suggests you aren't the sort to permit your marchioness to squander money on charity."

"I thought we already established my reputation is erroneous."

"So you claim." She folded her hands in her lap, unsure how to interpret their ride. He hardly knew her. He was a rake. Yet, he professed to care for her and wished to marry her. His rakish ways were a ruse or, at the very least, something he might set aside for her. It all seemed a bit difficult to believe.

She tightened her hands about each other, resisting the urge to raise one to her lips. Grace's advice had been terrible. Lanora's thoughts were not clearer. She still had no idea if she could believe Lord William, still doubted she wished a husband, in spite of her aunt's words. Now, though, the wants of her mind were clouded by a longing to feel his mouth on hers. She turned away, looking out over the park. Even his strong profile, glimpsed from the corner of her eye, tempted her. What had she done?

CHAPTER ELEVEN

William had a smile on his face and Lady Lanora in his thoughts as he strode up to Cecilia's door the following evening. A knock brought the maid. He hardly noticed her, hurrying upstairs to find his stepmother. He was in a rush, wanting to look into the foreman more before the theater. When he saw Lady Lanora there, he wished to have an answer for her. That she wouldn't expect one yet only gave the idea more appeal.

The street urchins would have located Finch's lodgings by now. Speaking to the foreman had gotten William nowhere. This time, he meant to search the man's rooms. He strode down the hall, walls blessedly unadorned, then came to a stop outside Cecilia's door and knocked.

"Come in."

She sat near the window, as usual, sewing. It took only a glance to see she was making over a gown. Sorrow touched him, as it always did when he was reminded how much she gave up, what life she missed, to stay safe. There was no choice. The marquess had already killed two wives.

She looked up with a smile, indominable as always. "You're early again. Does that mean you have letters for me?"

William pulled two envelopes from his coat with a bow, pleased to offer such happiness. "Your sister wrote, and your mother."

Setting aside her sewing, she jumped up, claiming the letters. "I should write him an extra letter. Perhaps with his ill health, he'll fall into a fit and die."

William knew she meant the marquess. Sending and receiving letters was a tricky business, for the marquess devoted considerable resources to locating his wife. Fortunately, William was up to the task of outsmarting the old man, though they'd agreed Cecilia would write only four times a year. Two of those times, she addressed messages to the marquess, to ensure he didn't declare her dead and remarry. Not to keep a hold on her title, but to spare another young woman. The letters enraged the old man.

"There'd be little harm in trying," he said.

"Will you sit?" Her smile was warm, but her hands clutched the letters.

"I will leave you to catch up on your family. I have it on good authority, the Mediterranean was exceptionally warm this past summer, if you care to mention it in your replies."

To preserve his reputation, the marquess told the world his wife suffered ill health that only the warmer southern climates could mitigate. William and Cecilia saw no reason to countermand the claim. William was certain, though, that most of Society at least suspected some other explanation for the continued absence of the marchioness. As he'd pointed out to Lethbridge, the old man's poor luck with wives was too suspicious to ignore.

Cecilia smiled. "Thank you. You're the most gracious stepson a woman ever had. Will I see you at breakfast?"

He shook his head. "I shall attend the theater. I hope to make the second act."

She nodded, making every attempt to hide her disappointment.

He knew her too well not to see it. "Tomorrow I shall visit longer, and tell you all about the theater. As much of it as I see, that is."

"It's kind of you, but I know you mustn't come too often or stay long. Who knows what your father will do if he worries you've fallen in love with your mistress or are disobeying his wish that you wed."

"I've taken enough steps toward courting one of the women on his list that I feel we're safe."

Her mouth rounded, her eyes lighting up. "Who? Do tell me."

"I'm sure it will be in the papers by tomorrow, as I took the lady for a ride in the park today and walked with her in the hedges."

"Did you now? How deplorable of you."

William grinned. "I'm a deplorable sort of fellow."

"Indeed. Especially if you make your own stepmother wait to read in the paper, who it is you're courting."

William knew her exasperation was feigned, but relented. "Lady Lanora Hadler."

"Lady…" Cecilia's eyes became as round as her mouth. "The archaeologist's daughter? She might know your friend Mr. Darington. How lovely."

William supposed it would seem so, to those who didn't know he'd never set foot in Egypt, never met Darington in person. He grinned, realizing that was how most of the *ton* would see it, making his courting Lady Lanora all the more believable.

Cecilia wrinkled her nose. "I don't mean offense, but I've read she's a diamond of the first water. A duke's only child who stands to inherit much in the way of lands and fortune. They say she's impeccable, even though she has black hair. How did you persuade her to ride with you in the park, let alone walk in the hedges?"

William's grin widened. "I, step-mama, am exceedingly charming."

Cecilia shook her head, expression amused. "I suppose you very well must be. Did you kiss her?"

"I'm shocked you would ask."

"Only because you're stung that I doubt your powers of seduction."

"True, but I still won't tell."

"Fair enough." Her look fond, she waved him away. "Go see to your mission."

"Don't forge—"

"To lock the doors." She settled into her chair. "I know. Good fortune out there."

"And a pleasant evening to you, my lady."

With another bow he quit the room, going to retrieve Lefthook's apparel and weapons. He grinned under his mask as he took in his reflection in Cecilia's mirror. Did Lady Lanora dream of Lord Lefthook, as so many ladies of the *ton* did? Should he go to the Solworth house, climb through her window, and make those dreams come true?

He chuckled, crossed to the Juliet balcony, and opened the doors. Lady Lanora was as like to push a man out her window as let him climb in. She had passion in her, waiting to be released, but what form it would take in the face of an intruder, he had little doubt.

His mind on her flashing green eyes, dark locks and other attributes, William set out across the rooftops. It took him some time scouring the streets before he located one of the urchins who lurked in the shadows of the borough. When he did, it was his favorite informant. The lad, a boy of about nine whom everyone called Dodger, was crouched in an alley, intently watching a door across the lane. William dropped down behind him, silent.

"Have you learned anything of interest for me?" he asked in lower London brogue.

Dodger didn't flinch, or take his attention from the doorway. "Can't you see I'm working, your lordship?"

William pulled out a coin. With a flip of his wrist, he sent it sailing over

Dodger's head to drop down before his face. The lad reached out and caught it, his gaze on the door.

The coin disappeared somewhere in his grimy clothes. "He's put up at Herald House, third window in from the left on the second floor, and he usually stays at the pub till it closes, your lordship."

"Good work," William said. As silently as he'd come, he returned to the rooftops.

Herald House was known for being nearly respectable. It stood on the edge of the borough, almost in a decent area. Not decent enough to have streetlamps, fortunately.

Once he reached the roof of Herald House, William lay silent for a time, listening. The London evening was dark, the low hanging smog bringing early night. William took in raucous laughter. Somewhere below, a child cried and a mother's voice soothed. A creaking wagon rolled by, drawn by a horse so old William didn't know if it would make it to the end of the street.

Eventually, deeming no one inside the third window in from the left on the second floor, he climbed down the side of the building. Bracing himself on the window ledge, he used his knife to slip open the latch on the shutters. As with many buildings in the borough, there was no glass. William slipped inside.

He stood still, allowing his eyes and ears to adjust. It was a single room, meant for sleeping and little else. Across from him was a door into the hall. There was no desk, but he could discern a small table piled with food scraps, empty bottles and a mug.

He crossed to the fireplace and stirred the coals, coaxing a bit of light from them. Staying near the wall so as not to be visible from outside, he went back around to the shutters and swung them shut. Then he began his search.

It wasn't long before a loose floorboard gave way to a heavy sack. Inside was enough coin for a man to live well in the borough for several months. It was not, however, enough to fund the building. William put coin, sack and board back in place. The foreman was likely skimming off the top, but the money he had didn't account for much of what was missing.

Further searching revealed nothing more, and William let the coals die. He would have to investigate Lethbridge's office tomorrow to ascertain if Darington's letters had ever arrived. His mind drifted back to the charred page in the grate, but he couldn't imagine Lethbridge as a thief. The man made a good living and was too much a toady. It took daring to steal. Lethbridge didn't have it in him. William shook his head. He would have no answers for Lady Lanora that night. Hopefully, his charming smile would be enough.

He went back out the window and hoisted himself onto the roof. He grinned as he made his way back across the rooftops, picturing Lady Lanora in his box with him at the theater, permitted by her apparently approving Aunt Edith to join him. Would Lanora be bold enough to steal kisses in the dark? She was brazen enough to request one in a sunlit garden.

An angry voice caught William's attention. He shook his head, clearing it of visions of Lady Lanora, and realized he was nearly back to the alley where he'd located his best informant earlier. He issued a silent curse, disgusted with his lack of attention. A man who wandered the borough with his head in the clouds was soon to be a dead man.

"I'm saying, she didn't come out this way." It was Dodger's voice, half angry, half distressed.

"She must have. My brother was watching the other side and he swears the chit didn't leave," a man growled. His accent labeled him as country born, and William didn't recognize his voice. Likely new to London, then.

"Then your brother's a liar."

"If you was really here all evening, where I hired you to be, you'll turn out your pockets. I know you didn't have a scrap on you when I left you here."

"My pockets are my own," Dodger said, but William could hear the fear in his voice.

"Turn 'um out or I'll shoot you dead and go through them before you're cold," the man said.

William slid to the edge of the roof overlooking the alley. He crouched there and peered over. Dodger was boxed in near the back of the alley, walls on three sides. A large, broken-nosed man stood between him and freedom, pistol at the ready. Dodger was shaking hard enough William could see it. Knowing the boy's pluck, William concluded the big man had already shown himself to be brutal.

"I'm telling you, I was watching all night till you came barging round," Dodger said.

The man shifted. He was about to shoot.

William launched himself over the edge as the pistol fired. He landed in front of Dodger. The bullet tore into William's side. Pain seared him, nearly mind-numbing.

"Bloody hell," the man barked. With a roar, he tossed his spent pistol and rushed William.

Reflex brought William's hands up. He ducked the onrush, pivoting away. The big man's momentum carried him past. His body behind the blow, William slammed his fist into the side of the man's head.

The big man stopped. He shook his head like a confused horse. William teetered. Hot blood ran down his side. He struck a second time. His fist slammed into the man's head, sending him over. He toppled, hitting the wall of the narrow alley. He slid along the brick and landed on his side with a thud.

Like a starved pup, Dodger leapt atop the body. Nimble fingers rummaged through the man's clothes, pulling out coins. He looked up, eyes bright. "That was something, your lordship. No one's ever done nothing like that for me before."

William took a staggering step backward, arm pressed to his side. He leaned against the opposite wall of the narrow alley. "Happy to oblige."

Dodger's hands stilled. "You hurt? He never landed a blow."

"I'm afraid his pistol did."

"You been shot?"

"It does seem that way." William forced himself away from the wall. It was a bloody wound. Deep. The bullet was still in there. He required skilled hands to remove it, and stitching. "If you've need of a few more coins, I have the feeling I'm going to require assistance."

At his side in a blink, Dodger looked up with a mixture of worry and devotion. "Anything you need, your lordship. Should I be taking you to the sawbones?"

"That won't be necessary." William would need to risk trusting this lad. He had to get back to Cecilia. She was the only person who knew his secret. She could mend him well enough. The trouble was reaching her chamber unseen. The marquess's spies were out front, servants within, and William was in no shape to climb anything, let alone leap between rooftops. "I have a place to go. I'll need your help to enter unseen, and your word you'll never tell a soul about where I'm going to take you."

"I can do that, your lordship." Dodger's expression became resolute. "You saved my life. No one's done nothing like that for me before. I'll see you're put right."

William nodded. He certainly hoped so.

CHAPTER TWELVE

Lanora woke peevish, which only made her more peevish. Why she'd expected Lord William to keep his promise of coming to the theater, she didn't know. Obviously, having gotten his kiss, he had no more use for her.

She rose and dressed as Mrs. Smith, while making every attempt to put his tall form, dark curls and mercurial hazel eyes from her thoughts. Mrs. Smith was due at the church to pass out food, and she had a purse of money for Mrs. Banke, to which she'd added a few coins. Lanora's life was too full for thinking about Lord William.

And his kiss.

"Good morning," Grace said, bustling into the room.

Three terriers followed her, or rather, the tray she carried. Grace knew Lanora was headed to the church early and wouldn't want to eat breakfast in the parlor dressed as Mrs. Smith. Even Aunt Edith would have the presence of mind to notice Lanora's grey hair.

Grace set the tray down and turned to Lanora, expression clouding. Behind Grace, the terriers lined up, noses pointed toward the table. "You look out of sorts."

"I'm perfectly well." Lanora reached for the powder.

Grace snatched up the jar and puff. "No, let me. You make such a mess."

"Then leave it for me to clean up," Lanora snapped.

Grace's eyes went wide. She set the powder back down with a thunk. "You *are* out of sorts. Whatever is the matter? You came home so dreamy-eyed from your ride, and seemed equally so when you left for the theater last night. Did I go to bed too early?"

Lanora pressed her lips together.

"Lanora?"

"I was not dreamy-eyed," she muttered. Not over Lord William Greydrake, rake and bounder.

"You were, and now you are not, and you've done your laces so tight, I think you shall faint."

Lanora rubbed at her chest. She did feel a bit faint. She'd been very aggressive in her tying, trying to stave off disappointment with anger. She'd such delightful ideas the whole ride to the theater, the whole first act, of sneaking into an alcove with Lord William. Why ask where she would be if he had no desire to see her?

"What happened at the theater?" Grace asked. She set the powder aside and began loosening Lanora's work.

"Absolutely nothing." Which was exactly the trouble. What if he'd only asked where she would be to ensure he did not see her again? A cold lump formed in her belly at the notion. She drew in a long breath, then let it out in a sigh. "Lord William said he would see me at the theater and he did not arrive."

Grace tilted her head to the side, considering. "Did he invite you to the theater?"

"No, I went with Aunt Edith, as planned."

"So he merely failed to show?"

After kissing her. "Yes."

"He may have a reason."

Lanora shrugged. "He may." Like, that he was out courting another unsuspecting woman.

"Shouldn't you let him give it before you become quite so…worked up?"

"Worked up?" Lanora frowned. "I do not get worked up."

"No, of course not." Grace's smile, glimpsed in the mirror over Lanora's shoulder, was faint. She retied the laces and took up the powder. "Sit down. You're too tall for me to do this with you standing."

With Grace's help, Lanora was soon ready. She ignored Grace's wish for her to eat, not being hungry, though she did offer the patient terriers a few tidbits. She went down the back stairs, for the servants all knew what she was about even if her aunt didn't, and left the townhouse to make her way to the church. A line had already formed outside the small building at the back. People greeted her as she went inside. The elderly priest stood within, passing out loaves.

"Father." Lanora offered a courteous nod. "I can do this. Thank you for not making them wait on me."

"Thank you for your work with the poor of London, Mrs. Smith. Send for me if you need me."

The old man shuffled away. Lanora stepped into the space he'd vacated behind the table. The morning passed slowly as she tried to hand out food with a pleasant demeanor, and not think of Lord William.

Distracted as she was, it was still a notable surprise when one of the street urchins she usually fed outside appeared before her table. "You've come in for bread." Lanora smiled a real smile, pleased she'd finally gained the trust of at least one of the boys.

"Lord Lefthook said you wasn't trying to cart me off and I should come in and make sure I got bread for me and my mates, so I'll be needing five loaves, Missus."

He looked about nine, as ragged and ill-kempt as all the urchins. She wondered if he'd really spoken to Lord Lefthook about her. "You know I can only give you one. It's the rule, with no exceptions."

"His lordship said you would say that, too, but can't I have just a few, Missus, for my mates?"

"You and Lord Lefthook are close, then?"

The boy's eyes brightened. He leaned over the table. "We're mates," he whispered, his gaze darting about, seeking eavesdroppers. "He saved me life last night. He took a bullet right in the side. For me." The boy made a dramatic gesture across his left side, along with a suitable, visceral grating, tearing sound.

"Did he?" Lanora was impressed, despite her inclination not to believe such silliness. "Well, that was grand of him, wasn't it? Then you two discussed me?"

The boy nodded. He puffed out his chest. "Was a long walk back to where he had to go, me helping him. We had a right cheery conversation. Bout all sorts of things. Me and him, like mates."

"Where he had to go? Where was that?"

He shook his head. "I can't say, and you can't say to no one that I told you any of that, or they'll try to beat it from me." He looked suddenly scared. "Can I have my bread, Missus? You won't say what I said to no one, will you? Lord Lefthook said you're a good sort."

Lanora composed her face into a solemn expression, though at least half of what the boy said was obviously flattery to get more bread. He'd likely sell it to his so-called mates. "I will not tell a soul." She held out two loaves. "If you can hide one of these right quick, so people see you walk out with only one, you may have both."

He snatched them up with a grin, one disappearing under his loose, ragged shirt, reinforcing her fear she'd been had. "Thank you, Missus. His lordship was right about you."

Lanora shook her head, but she couldn't be angry with the boy. Surely, he needed the extra coin the bread would bring him.

Peering out the door told her the line was almost gone, which was good because her supplies nearly were as well. The last person through the door was Mrs. Banke. Her eyes darted about in a way similar to the boy's as Lanora handed her a plump purse. She peered inside, a smile making her thin face almost pretty.

"Thank you, Missus." Mrs. Banke hugged the coins to her chest. "This is more than I'd hoped to get. It's a great help to me and my girl."

"Then I am glad." Lanora gathered up the few remaining loaves.

"You didn't tell no one, did you?"

She shook her head. These poor people, living in a world where getting the least bit ahead meant you had to fear every passerby. "I didn't breathe a word."

"Thank you, Missus."

Lanora held out a loaf. Mrs. Banke took it, clutching it nearly as tightly as the coins. Ducking her head, she scuttled away.

Lanora went outside, unsurprised to see the band of urchins lurking near the church, watching. What was striking was that many held small bits of bread, gnawing on them while they waited. The boy who'd come in was with them, hands empty. He grinned at her.

Bemused, Lanora set the six extra loaves of the day on the church steps. The boys didn't even wait for her to turn away before starting to inch forward. Wanting to reassure them, she left.

Heading toward the few rickety hired hackneys waiting in front of the church, Lanora pressed her lips together. Despite Mrs. Banke and the boy with his trust and his tale about Lord Lefthook, her mind would not give up dwelling on Lord William. She should go home, read, and never think of him again.

Instead, she hired one of the hackneys to take her to the address her footman had supplied. Lord William's mistress's home. Lanora wasn't sure what she would find there, but she felt almost driven to set eyes on the place. Maybe she would see this woman who so closely held Lord William's attention. Or, as it was still early for a gentleman, perhaps he would come stumbling out at some point, and she could confront him.

Recalling what her footman said about someone else watching Lord William, Lanora had the driver stop short of her destination. That seemed to suit him. He looked nervous to be in so nice an area, or maybe it was dropping a woman off on the street dubbed Mistress's Row.

She approached the intersection carefully, peering around the corner. The structure she sought was a perfectly lovely, if nondescript, townhouse. Curtains obstructed any view through the windows. Though that was normal, Lanora couldn't contain her suspicion. She glared at the building. Inside was a woman Lord William would rather spend time with than her.

Lanora pried her eyes away. She looked up and down the street. Across from the townhouse, a man lounged against a lamppost. He yawned. His garb was unremarkable, but his presence suspicious. It was obvious he had nothing to do but watch.

She settled against the corner and watched as well. At first, she worried the man would see her. It would be terribly embarrassing to be reported watching Lord William's mistress's home, but he never turned.

After about an hour, the day grew warm as the morning fog burned away to reveal a cloudless blue sky. Lanora was bored beyond endurance, and growing tired. After two hours, she was resolved. If the man watched, Lord William remained inside. Lanora would see him exit with her own eyes and try to catch a glimpse of the woman within. Surely, she would bid him farewell at the door. It seemed he was quite passionate about her, after all.

After around three hours, another plainly dressed man approached the first. They spoke a few words. The new one stayed. The other walked away.

Lanora looked back and forth between the two. She squared her shoulders. Neither had seen her. Other people walked the street. Mrs. Smith was not one to garner notice. She set off after the first man. If she wasn't going to learn anything by standing there, or see William, she would discover where this man went. Who else was having Lord William Greydrake followed? Knowing would tell her much.

The man didn't go to a residential district, as expected. Instead, he walked several blocks to an area of business. Frustration filled her. He was about his own tasks now. It would be hours before he returned to the person who'd sent him to spy.

He crossed the street and entered a building. She would have given up then, but she realized she knew the place. Or of it. It was the office of the attorney, Mr. Lethbridge. Mr. Darington's attorney. The one her father hadn't wanted. Intrigued, she hurried across the street. Was Mr. Darington having his onetime ward followed? Did that speak of disapproval for William's ways?

She entered in time to see the man turn at the top of the steps. She stopped, not sure what awaited her should she follow. Was her Mrs. Smith disguise enough to fool an attorney? She didn't believe she'd ever met Lethbridge. It seemed unlikely.

Squaring her shoulders, Lanora made her way up. She stepped boldly into the office. The smallish room, well-appointed but gloomy, was empty of people, the clerk's desk vacant. Voices sounded in the room beyond. She crept over and flattened herself against the wall beside the door behind the desk.

"…much longer," a cultured voice said. "Besides, I pay you well."

"Not that well. Watching that blighter is driving me mad." The man's voice was rough with a lower London accent. "Goes from one pleasure to the next. Don't know where the man finds the stamina. Slept in today, though, he did. Hasn't stirred from her house since yesterday evening. Chit must have worn him out last night."

"No doubt she learned he's courting Lady Lanora and wished to fortify her place in his regard."

Lanora nearly jumped at the sound of her name. She frowned. Courting her, was he? Not any longer.

"No doubt, indeed." The rough man chuckled.

"Have you seen her yet?"

"The mistress?" The man grunted. "Not hide nor hair. We're only there when he's there, and she don't go out when he's there. What'd be the point?"

"Still, it's odd. She can't know when he'll call round."

"Maybe he's got a standing appointment, like, or keeps his woman on a short leash. You want me to find someone to watch her, too? Cost you extra."

Short leash? What a thoroughly offensive term. Well, Lanora wouldn't be one of those women. Not ever. No. That's not needed. She's nothing."

"Suit yourself. So long as you pay me, and I don't go mad watching the blighter, it's all the same to me."

"Never fear. I can assure you this will all be resolved soon. Then you may return to your usual work, whatever that is."

The man's chuckle carried a nasty edge this time. "You don't want to know, Mr. Attorney."

"No, I do not. Now get out. I have another appointment coming."

Get out? Lanora's gaze darted around, landed on the clerk's desk.

"You're not closed up? Clerk's gone."

"I sent him home. My next appointment is private. Meaning you are to go. Now."

Lanora dove under the desk, pulling her skirt close. The chairs on either side, though difficult to dodge around, provided additional shelter.

"All right, I know where I'm not wanted."

Footsteps left the office and crossed the room. It wasn't until the man exited that she realized her error. If she'd simply taken a few steps across the room, she could have stood as if waiting for the clerk. It may have been suspicious, but not unduly so. She would simply have invented a legal matter and been sent packing, as Mrs. Smith obviously couldn't afford a man in this part of town.

Now, she was under a desk. Climbing out would take several seconds. If she was seen doing so, there would be no explaining how she got under there. At least the clerk had been sent home for the day. Hopefully, she could still sneak out, no one the wiser.

She tried to breath quietly, listening. In the office, papers moved. The attorney, Mr. Lethbridge, muttered to himself. Lanora started to ease out one of the chairs. Footsteps clattered on the steps. She eased the chair back closer. A heavy tread entered.

"Lethbridge?" It was another man with a lowborn accent. Did Mr. Lethbridge specialize in spying for the wealthy?

"In here. Close the outer door."

Lanora heard the door click shut. She winced. The heavy footsteps entered Mr. Lethbridge's office. She rested her chin on her knees. If Grace could see her, she'd be horrified, but she'd also laugh. It was like Lanora to get into such an intractable situation.

"How is the building business, Finch?"

Finch? That was the name of the foreman directing the building of the home for displaced women. Lanora was suddenly glad of her place under the desk.

"You mean the not-building business?" Finch said, his voice recognizable now that she'd heard his name.

"Exactly."

"People been asking questions. You ever going to give me the funds? That Darington fellow wrote me direct, you know. I'm pretending I can't read, but he'll figure it's you, eventually. You aren't paying me enough to hang for you."

"I told you, the money is tied up. I made some rather…questionable investments. I have a fortune coming to me soon, though."

Mr. Lethbridge had used Darington's funds?

"If you say so, Lethbridge," Finch said. "I can't see no one handing you a fortune, though."

"No one needs to hand it to me. I'm going to take it, in the form of an heiress soon to come under my control. If you have any notion how impressionable sixteen-year-old girls are, you know she'll be mine soon enough, and a marquess's fortune with her."

"If you don't mind me saying, I can't see no pretty young thing agreeing to wed you either, impressionable or no."

"She will. It will be me or no man. I'll see she's unfit for anyone else, if it comes to it."

Lanora's mouth dropped open, but she quickly shut it. Was Mr. Lethbridge talking about compromising some poor young woman about to become his ward, forcing her to marry him and using her money to pay off his debts? The fiend. She had to discover who the unfortunate girl was and put a stop to his despicable plan.

"You do what you have to, Lethbridge," Finch said. "Just wanted you to know people been asking questions. I'll need that money before long."

"Use some of what I paid you to stop building to start back up. I'll replace it."

"I don't think so. Get me the funds before Darington sends the watch after me, or I'll talk and you'll swing."

"Yes, fine, you have made your point. Was that all?"

"All I have to say."

"Then get out, and try not to come here. It's suspicious. People will see you."

Finch grunted. Footsteps crossed the room again. The door opened. Lanora stayed as still as she could, her mind reeling.

What sort of man took his client's money, slated to build a home for women, and lost it, then plotted to seduce some innocent girl given into his care? And none of it explained why Mr. Lethbridge was having Lord William followed. Lanora finally understood the lack of progress on the women's home, but so many new questions had sprung up to replace that conundrum.

She realized the sounds of muttering and paper shuffling had increased. Mr. Lethbridge came out of his office, closed the door, and crossed the room. Her heart thudded. The outer door shut and a key turned in the lock. After a shocked moment of silence, she slipped from beneath the desk. She ran to the door, but it wouldn't open. She was trapped.

CHAPTER THIRTEEN

William strode up to the door of Lethbridge's building, relying on the dark to obscure him from casual observation. He cast a look up and down the street, finding it empty. He would have preferred gaining entry via the window, clad as Lefthook, but when it came to the wealthier parts of town, future marquess was a better disguise than vigilante of the poor. If it came down to it, he could pretend inebriation to explain his presence where he didn't belong. His title would take care of the rest.

Not that he was in any shape for climbing in windows, which had impeded evading the marquess's surveillance. He'd done well enough for a man who'd hardly been able to climb the servants' stairs the night before. In truth, the most difficult task of his day thus far had been convincing Cecilia he was fit enough to go out. If she had her way, he would have remained in bed

William would have given in to his stepmother's coddling, but he needed to find out what was going on with the home for women. He knew, in view of his reputation, Lanora would think the worst about his absence at the theater. He wanted something to show for it before he saw her again, to make it up to her.

Assured the street was empty, William dug out a set of lock picks and let himself in. The door to Lethbridge's office was a similarly surmountable barrier. He closed it softly behind him.

Once inside, William used memory to reach the fireplace, and stirred up the coals for light. He went from the reception room into Lethbridge's office, finding that door open. Oddly, so was the narrow door at the back of the room, the one protecting Lethbridge's records. In all his visits to the attorney's office, he had never seen that door open. Intrigued, he checked that the curtains were closed and coaxed a larger flame from the grate. Assured the room was secure from escaping light, he pulled out several candle stubs and lit them.

Something slid softly across the floor in the reception room. There was a rustle of fabric. Quiet footsteps sounded. They seemed to be moving away from him, but it was hard to tell from the faint sounds. Hand on his pistol, William whirled.

"Lady Lanora?" he blurted, stunned.

She turned, appearing equally shocked. Her hair, showing lingering evidence of powder, was half down. Now that William thought to look for them, he noted several bent hairpins on the desk. She held a single page clutched in her hand. Her expression made a rapid switch from shock to cold anger.

"Lord William." She strode toward him, shoulders back and chin up. "Perhaps you can explain this." She slapped the page down on Lethbridge's desk.

What in God's name was Lady Lanora Hadler, dressed in her lowly widow's costume and looking thoroughly disheveled, doing in Lethbridge's office? Hot rage shot through William as he took in the details of her wrinkled gown and disarrayed tresses. He recalled her mention of hairpins.

"What are you doing here? What is the meaning of these?" He pointed to the hairpins.

She spared them a glance. "I was attempting to release the catch and let myself out."

Let herself out? "Nothing more dire or...scandalous?"

"Don't be ridiculous." She sounded as angry as he was. "Now you tell me, what is this?" She tapped the page.

William dropped his gaze, trying to rein in his emotions. Shouting was unlikely the best course. She certainly appeared unharmed. She still tapped the page she'd slapped down on the desk. He focused on it. The marquess's list of potential wives for William. With his signature at the bottom. She had the damn list.

Composing himself, he strove for something resembling his easy, usual manner. He leaned a hip against the desk, suppressing a wince of pain. The stitched-up hole in his side gave a bloody good impression of a knife stab. "That's an interesting ensemble, my lady."

"How I choose to dress is none of your concern, my lord. Nor will it ever be." Her lips pressed into a thin line. It was a shame to abuse them so, denying their lushness. "Now explain yourself."

William rubbed the back of his neck. Was there any way to distract her? "Explain myself? Does it occur to you that you're in an attorney's office, alone, in the dark?" He grinned and looked her up and down. "Well, not alone anymore."

Her eyes grew as narrowed as her lips. She took up the page and shoved it in front of his face. "Explain this."

No, there would be no distracting her. William grimaced. "It's a list." He plucked the page from her fingers and placed it behind him.

"I can see it's a list. What is it a list of?" She put a hand to her head. "If you say names, I shall retrieve another pin and stab you."

"The marquess has bid me marry. He had Lethbridge draw up a list of suitable candidates."

She paled, hand dropping. "I see. So, all your talk of watching me from afar, that was a lie."

"It most certainly was not. No man could help but admire your beauty."

"And your talk of not truly being a rake, not carrying on with your mistress. Lies." She'd gone so cold as to appear emotionless.

"Nothing I've said to you is a lie. I omitted my reason for pursuing you now, at this time. That doesn't mean I don't esteem you. The timing has nothing to do with my feelings for you."

A thread of desperation snaked through him. Now that he knew her, Lady Lanora was the only possible choice. He couldn't let her refuse him. Even his daydreams of Darington's daughter waned in comparison to the reality of Lanora. He would not select another name. No other would ever do.

"Of all the names on that list, yours is the only one that ever interested me. I swear."

She was so pale, even her lips lacked color. "And if my name did not appear on that list, would you have pursued me?"

He went still. How could he answer that? She was the one woman he'd avoided above all others.

"I read your answer in your face, my lord. I think we are done here."

She turned on her heels, regal even in her dowdy garb. She was walking away from him. Leaving. William felt a surge of panic. He blinked rapidly, confused by such a foreign emotion.

"Stop." That single word, harsher and louder than he intended, stood alone in the space between them. She turned back. His heart started beating again.

"Why?" She folded her arms across her chest.

She's hurt, he realized. The pain of betrayal shown in her green eyes. If she was hurt, she must care for him. "Because I love you." The words, pulled from him in desperation, rang exultantly true.

Her mouth dropped open. She stared at him for a lifetime. William locked his gaze with hers, willing her to see the truth of his declaration.

"You... What did you say?" she asked, the question breathless.

Three long strides brought him to her. "I love you, Lanora. I didn't mean to. I picked your name off the list because of your father, I admit that. Because he knows Darington, and that interested me." With a finger under her chin, he tilted her face up toward his. "I won't lie. If I don't marry by the marquess's deadline, he will sign his fortune over to my sister, a girl of sixteen. I can't let that happen. Not for my sake, but for hers, and that of so many others. I have plans for the marquess's money. The shelter Darington is funding is only the start. I want to help people, Lanora."

"The shelter for women?" She looked dazed. "Lethbridge took the money. I overheard him, but I couldn't find anything. No letters from Darington, at all." She shook her head, taking a half step back. "You're using me to secure your father's fortune? I suppose you wouldn't mind having mine as well."

"No." He closed the distance between them again. "That isn't the way of it."

She kept shaking her head. "I don't believe you. You're a rake."

Never had William regretted his reputation more. "I'm not. I swear. I can prove it." He could. He would. "I correspond with Darington. He's one of two people in this world who knows who I really am." Revealing Cecilia was not his right. He wouldn't put her in danger, even if it broke his heart. "I'll bring you his letters. You'll see what sort of man he finds me to be. Surely, you'd take his word? He's your father's partner."

"No. Perhaps." She looked up at him, features taut with despair. "I don't know what to believe."

"Believe this." He covered her lips with his, needing to feel the heat they'd shared in the park, to rekindle it.

Her response was instant. Her lips pliant, soft. He crushed her to him, ignoring the pain that shot out from his side. She wrapped her arms about his neck. He raked his fingers through her hair, sent the remaining pins flying. Dark locks tumbled free. He buried a hand in their silkiness and cupped her neck, pressing her closer.

She slid her palms down his chest, then between them. A sudden push, one hand braced over the bandages she didn't know were there. William stumbled back. Pain at the loss of her proximity and esteem mixed with the physical agony her shove woke in his side.

"No." Her breath came in ragged gasps. "I won't...you can't kiss me. You don't love me and we will never marry." She turned and ran.

William started after her, grimacing in pain. He shook his head, unsure which hurt more, her declaration or the bullet wound.

Lanora disappeared through the door at the base of the stairs as he started down. On the street, she ran to the end. William gritted his teeth, lengthening his stride. Each step jarred the gunshot wound. Pain stabbed through him. He followed her around a corner, watched her climb into a hired hackney. It pulled away.

He retreated back around the corner and leaned against the wall. She would get home safe. The drivers in the area were respectable.

"You need help, your lordship?" a piping voice asked.

William looked down to find Dodger, face smudged with dirt. "You followed me from Chastity's?"

"A sight better than that other bloke. Don't worry, you lost him a ways back." The boy crinkled his face in thought. "Is Chastity your pretty lady friend who lives in the house? You never did say her name, which isn't good manners, your lordship."

William closed his eyes. He hoped he hadn't errored in trusting Dodger with the location of Cecilia's home. "Yes, and you're never to speak of her. To anyone. Her life is forfeit should she be found."

"Who'd hurt a pretty lady like that? She was like an angel, all lovely like and kind. She gave me food, you know, after we was done stitching you up. You're Lord William Greydrake, aren't you, lordship?"

William sighed. He pushed himself off the wall and started back toward Lethbridge's. Dodger trotted along beside him. Lethbridge's office needed to be put right. William doubted there was any point to searching for Darington's letters about the home for women. Lanora's words, coupled with the remnants he recalled seeing in the grate, made finding them unlikely.

"I won't tell anyone you're Lefthook, lordship. Not a soul," Dodger said as they climbed the steps back to Lethbridge's office. "You can count on me."

William looked about the room, eyes drawn to the strewn hairpins. Through the second door, he could see closed curtains, his candle stubs burned low. The slightly wrinkled page still lay on the desk, silently accusing. His evening had not gone as planned.

"I believe I can count on you, Dodger. Would you help me complete a few tasks here before we lock up? I don't mean to harp on my good deed, but I daresay chasing after a lady wasn't the best kind of wound treatment."

"Right away, your lordship." The boy didn't move, but watched him.

"What is it, Dodger? You can ask. I won't be angry."

Dodger looked about the room. "It's just, that lady who ran out, she looked a lot like Mrs. Smith. We all like her. You like her. You said she's a good sort."

"That's true." If only she liked him, life would be perfect.

"She ran off awful upset, looking a sight." Dodger looked down. "You didn't, that is, you didn't hurt Mrs. Smith in any way, did you, your lordship?" The boy looked up, eyes wide. "Only, I'll still keep your secrets, I swear it, but I won't be helping you if you hurt that lady."

William smiled, though the expression felt pained. Dodger was a good sort, too. "I did no physical harm to the lady. I'm afraid I may have done some to her heart, though, and mine."

Dodger looked confused. "Her heart? Like, love and such?"

"Exactly like love and such. You see, I love the lady. I believe she may care for me, but, at the moment, she's very cross with me."

Dodger made a vague gesture around the room. "Them's a lot of hairpins for a broken heart, your lordship."

William chuckled, then winced. "Yes, well, we may have kissed, but I assure you, that was all. I would never harm that lady. I mean to marry her."

"You intend to marry the Widow Smith?"

"It's a bit more complicated than that, but yes, I mean to. If she'll have me."

"If you say so, lordship." Dodger shook his head, looking doubtful.

"Will you help me?"

"Yes, your lordship. I don't think you're the type would hurt a lady, anyhow. I wouldn't have asked had she not looked so distressed."

William nodded. "You're a good lad, Dodger."

With the boy's help, he set to work.

CHAPTER FOURTEEN

*L*anora took the steps of the servant's staircase two at a time. Tears burned her eyes. She couldn't tell if they were of anger or fatigue. They weren't from sorrow, for she'd lost nothing in William's betrayal. She'd known from the start he was a rake and not the man she would wed. No man was. She would live like her aunt. The people she and her father watched over would simply have to hope their new lords were worthy when Lanora ended their branch of the Solworth line, childless.

She managed to gain the security of her room before tears fell in earnest. Collapsing on her bed, she let them well forth with bitter sobs. She didn't want to die childless. She wanted William's son. A lively, mischievous boy who would be nearly more trouble than he was worth, but with the heart of an angel. She wanted William's arms about her. His kiss. The security of his love.

She slammed a fist down on the coverlet. She would never have that security. He'd selected her name from a list. She hadn't even been at the top. An afterthought, near the end. She hated that page, with its coldly drawn up list of only the wealthiest, most desirable young women. She hated William's signature, so bold at the bottom, but smudged as if written by someone who used their left hand. His signature was like the rest of him, perfection artfully disarrayed.

"Lanora." Grace burst into the room.

Lanora lifted her head, taking in her friend's red-rimmed eyes.

Grace rushed to her and pulled her into a hug. "Where have you been? I've been beside myself with worry. This is all my fault, for letting you go off alone. What happened?"

Lanora drew in a long, shuddering breath, hugging Grace back. "Nothing. Nothing really. Does my aunt know I was missing?"

Grace let go, holding Lanora at arm's length to look her over. "Nothing? Your hair is a mess. Your gown is wrinkled. You're crying." Grace's eyes flew wide. Her face drained of color. "My God. Your hair, your gown...Lanora, you didn't."

"Didn't what?" She blinked several times, trying to clear her thoughts.

"You've gone and let your virtue go." Grace heaved a sob. "Oh no. Oh, this is not good."

"What? I most certainly have not." Lanora looked down at her dress, creased from her time hiding under the desk. She pushed at her hair, though there was little hope of achieving any order. The few remaining pins fell out. "Grace, listen to me. I didn't give up anything. Don't cry so."

Grace grabbed her arm and pulled her across the room. She shoved Lanora in front of her mirror. "Look at you."

She did look awful. She could understand Grace's fear. "Honestly, I haven't given up my virtue."

"Then where have you been? What happened? I told your aunt you're too ill to go out. She didn't say anything, but even the dogs looked suspicious. I know they could tell I was lying."

"I can explain." Letting out a sigh, Lanora returned to the bed and settled on the edge. "I didn't tell you, but I kissed Lord William when we were in the park. Once." She offered a glare. "Which was your idea, if you'll recall." She paused, organizing her thoughts. "Then, when he didn't come to the theater as he said he would, I was…angry."

Grace was dabbing at her eyes with a handkerchief. "You kissed him? How could you not tell me? So, it was a good kiss? You must have learned you care for him, or you wouldn't have been so out of sorts this morning."

"I do not care for him."

"Do you really believe that?"

"You will as well, once you hear all." Lanora looked down. Grace was not going to like the next part. "After handing out bread this morning, I went to spy on Lord William, at his mistress's house. I wanted to confront him when he came out."

"Lanora." That single word held a wealth of disappointment.

"He never came out. Nor did she. Someone else was watching for him too, though, just as Joseph reported. When the man watching the house left, I decided to try to learn who else cared where Lord William went."

Grace stood with her hands on her hips, glaring. Lanora realized her days of going out alone as Mrs. Smith were over. From the look on Grace's face, it would take all of Lanora's persuasiveness to keep her aunt from being informed of her behavior.

"The man went to an attorney. I followed him in and eavesdropped."

Grace threw up her hands. Her tears were dry now, scorched away by her anger. "Lanora."

Lanora winced. "It gets worse. I had to hide under a desk, so I wouldn't be seen. That's how I ended up locked in the attorney's office. I was trapped."

"By all that's holy, Lanora."

"I know, it was bad, but I did learn a lot." Bitterness laced her tone.

"Let me have a bath drawn up in your dressing room and you can tell me what you learned. We have to get you cleaned up."

"I can help."

"You cannot." Grace's expression turned to one of alarm. "No one saw you come in looking like this, did they? None of the others?"

Lanora shook her head. "I don't think so."

"Let's pray not." Grace pivoted and hurried from the room.

Lanora organized her thoughts while Grace worked in the adjoining room, readying a tub. Lanora could hear other members of the staff come and go, some asking after her health in soft tones. Grace's relief sounded real when she told them Lanora would be well soon. Lanora hadn't meant to distress Grace so, and for what? Though she'd told Grace she'd learned a lot, what had she really learned? One thing, at least, that was important. The attorney Mr. Darington used, the one her father hadn't wished to employ, had stolen the funds for the women's home. There was no other way to put it. He'd appropriated them and then lost them, somehow.

She'd found no written evidence of that, however. No records of Darington at the attorney's, at all. There was one more place to look, though. A strongbox hidden in the wall, behind a painting hung over the mantel. Lanora suspected Lethbridge had selected the dullest landscape he could find so the painting would garner little attention. The strongbox behind it was the only part of the office that had resisted her search, for search she had. She'd plenty of time, after all, locked in for hours.

She knew she could get into the strongbox if she brought her lock pics. She was quite skilled at picking locks, for all she hadn't been able to fashion the right tools by bending her hairpins. She used to practice the skill for hours. In her child's mind, Egyptian treasure was sealed in chests, like pirate gold, and once she'd convinced her father to take her with him on his expeditions, she would have shown him her talent. That childish fancy would serve her well now. If she was going to bring Lethbridge to justice and see the home for women finished, she would need to go back and look in that strongbox.

Lanora rose and slowly began to undress. Grace was correct, her garments were uncommonly wrinkled. Lanora was sure Grace would wash them herself. It wouldn't do for the others to suspect that Lanora had done anything compromising, for even loyal servants gossiped. Lanora paused. What could Lord William possibly have been doing in Lethbridge's office in the middle of the night? She'd heard him at the door. She would wager her father's fortune he'd picked the lock. Had he learned that skill in Egypt? To her dismay, her father assured her Egyptians used much more elaborate mechanisms.

How didn't matter as much as *why*, though. Why was Lord William there? What was he looking for at the attorney's? Perhaps the list? Although she had no idea why he might worry it would be circulated, it was certainly incriminating. He could have gone there to secure it. She wished he'd done so before she set eyes on it.

Lanora stop undressing, then crossed to the fire and stirred it up to ward off the chill in her room. No, she didn't wish he'd hidden the list. It was good she'd seen it. She couldn't live in a dream world, because one always woke up. Better the pain in her heart now than waking up to find herself married to Lord William, while he spent Lanora's fortune on his mistress.

She frowned, tugging free her laces. It was all so odd, though. Lethbridge having Lord William followed. His mysterious mistress no one ever saw. His claims that his father was making him marry. His father making him pretend to be someone he was not, a cold, cruel, ruthless, cad of a man. Could she believe any of it?

Well, she believed the part about being ordered to marry. That explained how she'd become mixed up in Lord William's life. Watched her from afar, indeed. How had she ever considered believing that?

Lanora let out a sigh, stepping from the ring of clothing at her feet. She'd started to believe it because she wished to. He was handsome. Warm. So convincing. It would be terribly nice to have a man like the one he pretended to be love her as he pretended to love her.

She blinked, recalling what else she'd overheard. Pretend love. Was that a weapon of all men? She doubly needed to return to Mr. Lethbridge's office. She had to learn who this poor girl was he would soon be guardian to. Lanora would not let Mr. Lethbridge seduce or coerce some young woman into marrying him.

Once the other staff left, she would tell Grace all she'd learned that evening. Even Grace must agree there were worthy reasons for returning to Mr. Lethbridge's office to search. And if Grace didn't agree, well, Lanora would have to be sneaky.

CHAPTER FIFTEEN

William spent another night at Cecilia's, enduring her dismay at his somewhat weakened state, secretly relieved to have someone coddle him. He knew he shouldn't have gone out so soon after being shot. Even sitting up in bed pained him. He couldn't help but wish, as Cecilia tended him, that he could go to a different woman for care. One who would likely berate him rather than offer sympathy, but whose touch would surely soothe her harsh words.

He and Cecilia also discussed, and agreed, that Chastity must go. As William had spent two nights and much of a day with Chastity, there was no way to combat the marquess's suspicion other than getting a new mistress. For lack of a better name, and in the hopes this would be a short-lived incarnation, they would use her choice of Valentina.

William returned to his townhouse directly following breakfast. He bathed carefully and dressed himself. Even with his wild ways, he would be hard pressed to explain a bullet wound to his valet, who would convey the information to the marquess.

Suitably attired, William retired to his office. There, he wrote a letter to Lethbridge, informing him he was turning out Chastity. He'd already met a new lover, an up and coming Italian opera singer. Valentina was only an understudy, but William found her attributes pleasing.

He informed Lethbridge new servants would be required, and a sum for Chastity, as a parting gift. He added to that a request for livery for Dodger. William meant to take the boy in, if he'd agree. The livery he requested immediately, along with letting the old servants go, with compensation.

The date for hiring new ones, William left open. Cecilia would have Dodger, hopefully, and always enjoyed a few days on her own. Servants were a strain, for any one of them could turn into a spy if they came across the right information. Making a fuss about moving Valentina in wasn't necessary. The request alone would shore up the hole in their defenses.

Next, his thoughts grim, William wrote to Darington. He informed his friend of Lethbridge's deceit. He knew he'd only Lanora's slightly garbled words to go on, but they rang true. That was the reason for the burned letter in the grate. That was why the funds Darington requested hadn't gone toward construction.

William should have realized Lethbridge's duplicity sooner. It seemed inconceivable the man would steal, though. He had a secure position and took in a good living. Why risk that? Then, some men were slaves to ambition, and Lethbridge was a second son. They often felt slighted by life.

Those tasks complete, William unlocked the drawer containing his letters from Darington. Nearly twelve years of missives. At first, William had kept them for their details of Egypt, to be reread to bolster his memory of his subterfuge. Later, he began keeping them because Darington was his one true friend, aside from Cecilia. One could get only so close to a young woman, though, especially one's own stepmother, and William had never admitted his greatest secret to her, that he'd never been to Egypt.

William took the most recent letters from the drawer. Contained therein was much about the women's home. That should paint him in a favorable light. Darington also spoke of his daughter, at length, in most of his letters, extolling her virtues.

A wistful smile played across William's mouth. Darington's daughter. A lost dream. A kind, intelligent, accepting, loving woman. Was she even real?

He shook his head. She was, but not for him. The reality of Lanora scattered that dream. He hoped Darington's daughter would find a good man. One she actually knew. Someone to love her.

William tucked the letters into his coat, standing. He gripped the side of the desk, grimacing in pain. Moving with a bit more care, he went to request his carriage.

He arrived at the Solworth townhouse in good spirits. He would show Lanora the letters. She would read them and see the truth. William was a good man. Her father's partner obviously thought so. They discussed weighty and important things with candor. Among them, ways to better the lives of London's poor. Lanora would see how nearly she and William were allied.

Perhaps then, once she could see him for who he was, he would reveal all to her. He'd lived on the streets. He was Lord Lefthook. He cared more for the fate of those same women and children she wished to help than for his own class. How his mother had died.

No, not that. He would shelter Lanora from the truth of the marquess's evil. There would be no talk of his mother, Charles or either of his stepmothers. It was too dark to share, and the marquess still lived. While he did, Cecilia would never be safe. Resolved, William strode up the steps and knocked.

"May I help you, my lord?" asked the stern-faced butler who opened the door.

William glanced around, wondering where the cheerful maid of last time was. This man seemed much more formidable. "Lord William Greydrake for Lady Lanora."

"Her ladyship is not at home." The man didn't blink.

"Not at home?"

"No, my lord. May I take your card?"

William frowned. She must be home. It wasn't one of the days Dodger said she passed out bread as Mrs. Smith. She had no friends. From her talk of slippers, and all else he knew of her, he imagined she found shopping frivolous. "Not home, or not at home to me?"

"Precisely, my lord."

"I see." William took out his card and handed it over. "Please tell her I called."

"Yes, my lord."

He permitted the man to close the door. He wouldn't embarrass her by telling her butler he had letters to show her. That was highly inappropriate. Nor would he make a scene in her foyer. He was in no shape to be forcing his way inside. No, he would have to resort to bribery.

Returning to his carriage, he had his driver take him around the corner. Once there, William disembarked and made his way to the back of the townhouse on foot. The day wasn't too warm, fortunately, the sky dotted with clouds. When he reached Solworth House, the locked garden gate was no obstacle to him. Closing it behind him, he turned to find six terriers watching.

Taking care of his side, he dropped to one knee on the stone walk, holding out his hands. "Come here, you lot. You remember me."

They trotted nearer, only the Skye Terrier lingered out of reach. He watched for a long moment, assessing, as William petted the others. Finally, he turned and meandered away, plopping down in the shade of a bush.

"So, I may pass?" William asked. He took the lolling tongues as a yes, and stood.

Peering around a line of hedges, he sighted a round-faced kitchen maid seated in the sun, shucking peas. He was in luck. Maids were generally quite willing to part with information for a few spare coins.

Adopting an expression that proclaimed he was wealthy enough to walk where he wished, William strode around the corner. Several of the pups followed. "Good afternoon."

The young woman looked up with a start. She set the bowl aside, standing. "You don't belong here."

William was a bit taken aback by the hard edge to her country lilt. Obviously, a show of rank was needed. Being country bred, she likely didn't recognize the quality of his clothing, or attitude. Perhaps he should have gone with charm instead of command, but he was loath to flirt with any woman who wasn't Lanora.

"I beg your pardon? Have you any notion to whom you speak?"

She tipped her head to the side, looking him up and down. Her eyes went wide. "Are you Lord William, then?"

"I am."

The young woman stepped forward and slapped him.

The force of the blow turned his head. Country bred, indeed. William rubbed his jaw. "Have we met?"

"How dare you kiss Lanora and then stand her up? What game are you playing? Do you know how hard her aunt and I have worked to convince her to even consider the notion of wedding?"

William felt he was missing something. He considered her for a long moment. A common kitchen maid. That's what she appeared to be. Yet... "Grace?"

Table turned, she gave him a look of surprise. "I am."

"Lanora's dearest friend, who suggested she kiss me?"

Grace blushed. "Before I learned about your bloody awful list of names."

Lanora's dearest companion was a kitchen maid? She truly didn't have any friends. No wonder she didn't wish them to meet. She was likely embarrassed, just as she would be of William if he ever told her the whole truth. Fear snaked through him. She would find out eventually. If he won her now, would she leave him then? He didn't care. He couldn't give her up.

"I have an explanation for the list."

"That you need a wealthy bride to secure your fortune. So I heard."

"That is not the whole of it," William snapped, angered Lanora had shared so much. Grace must truly be her dear friend. Had Lanora told her everything?

"Oh, she said you tried to explain it all away. I'm sure you can be very convincing, my lord, especially when you're kissing a girl."

"She told you about our second kiss, then?" Her betrayal cut, angered him. "I suppose you had a good laugh over my declaration of love?"

Her jaw went slack. She looked almost as flabbergasted as Lanora had. "Your what?" she squeaked.

William rocked back on his heels, reining in his hurt. He pushed a hand through his hair. "My declaration of love."

Grace shook her head. She sank back down onto the bench. A terrier jumped up beside her. Absently, she patted the shaggy head. "No wonder she was so upset. I haven't seen Lanora cry like that since she realized her father was never going to let her join him in Egypt."

The image of a young Lanora, dreams of salvaging what little family remained to her shattered, lodged in his heart. The sting of her betrayal disappeared.

Grace shot him a suspicious glance. "At first, I thought you'd done more to her than kiss her. I was ready to hunt you down, if you don't mind me saying."

"Not at all. I'm happy to know someone would have." He meant it. At least someone cared what happened to Lanora, aside from him. "May I?" he added, seating himself on the other side of the bowl of peas. A dog plopped down by his feet.

"You love her?" Grace repeated, scrutinizing him.

William eased back against the bench, mindful of his bandaged side. "I do."

"You only just met her."

He shook his head. "So she's repeated often enough."

"Are you certain you love her? I gather you're more accustomed to easy conquests. It could simply be the novelty of a woman who says no."

"I am positive that I love her, nor have I ever had such illusions before. She is the first." Aside from Darington's daughter, but that was love of a dream. He stretched his legs out before him. "She is all elegance and beauty, but inside she has spirit. She pretends to be above everyone, even other nobles, but she dresses as a widow and feeds the poor in the worst slum of London. Apparently, she also breaks into attorney's offices. What is there not to love about a woman like that?"

Grace eyed him for a long moment. "Lady Edith says you're a good man.

She says it's a wonder how much of your mother she sees in you, since you only knew her until you were four."

William looked down at his hands. "Lady Edith compliments me. My mother was a wonderful woman."

"She went mad, or so people say."

He clenched his jaw over a rejoinder. He drew in a steadying breath. "People say much that isn't true."

"Aye. They do, at that." She nodded, as if making up her mind. "You're here to see Lanora."

"I am. I wasn't permitted in. I came around back to attempt bribing a servant to tell me where she will be next."

"Not very noble of you."

"I don't claim to be noble. I claim to be in love." Each time he said it, it became more real, hurt more. The only way to salve that pain was to have Lanora in his arms.

"You wouldn't have had any luck. We all love her like family. We are family. My mum, the duke's housekeeper on his country estate, raised Lanora right alongside me. Before you can be sure you love her, you should know that." Grace's tone was earnest. "At home, we all take our meals together in the kitchen. She gardens, and she usually helps me with the peas. She goes to country dances. She's not like other ladies. If that's not what you want, you won't be happy with her."

William closed his eyes. It sounded like heaven. It was how Darington described his daughter. Kind to the very center of her being. Noble of heart. Knowing people for who they truly were, not what title they held. Not embarrassed of Grace, then. Afraid of his judgement, as he was of hers. Perhaps, even, a woman who could know his truth.

"I must speak with her. Please, let me see her."

"She's truly not in. She went for a ride in the park."

William shot to his feet, pain coursing through his side. "A ride in the park? Who dared ask her?" He glared down at Grace. From the corner of his eye, he caught a reproachful look from the dog who'd settled near his toes.

Grace was slack jawed for a brief moment, then a smile spread across her face. "Lady Edith. She's riding with her aunt."

"Ah, my apologies. I thought..." William tugged at his cravat. It was obvious what he thought. There was no reason to say aloud that his mind had instantly conjured an image of Lanora in the flower garden with another man.

Grace stood, her eyes sympathetic. "Go home for now, my lord. Give me this evening to speak with her. I promise, she'll be in when you call tomorrow."

"You'll champion my cause?"

"I believe I will." Grace's smile widened to reveal dimples. "And with me on your side, you can't help but prevail."

CHAPTER SIXTEEN

"I'm not sure." Lanora tried to sit still at her dressing room table, to contain her nervousness.

"I am. You must speak with him. I've rarely seen a gentleman so besotted." Grace stood behind her, making final adjustments to Lanora's midnight tresses, artfully arranged and dotted with small crystals.

"And you told him about me? About how I'm friends with you, and that in the country we're all like family, and that I shall not change for a man?"

Grace rolled her eyes. "I said as much."

"And he didn't back down? He didn't rescind his love?" Could it be true? Her heart, a broken-winged bird fluttering in her chest, longed for the balm of William's love. If he really loved her, she could forgive him the list. He was correct. It mattered not if he'd selected her from a list at the behest of his father. What mattered was the love they'd found after that selection was made.

If he loved her. If any of it was real. He'd charmed Grace, that was clear. That didn't mean he wasn't a cad who needed her to marry him to keep his fortune, gaining her father's in the process. In that case, what difference did it make to him if he pretended to accept her eccentricities? Likely, once they were wed, he'd have her locked away in a mental institute as his father had his mother.

"Why was he in Lethbridge's office? I know he broke in," Lanora said, a worry she'd already voiced several times.

"You shall have to ask him. I daresay he'll answer. He seems forthcoming."

He often did. Yet, she always felt he was holding back, as well. Sometimes he seemed evasive.

"Besides, you don't know that he broke in. You suspect. You expect me to believe you can tell the difference between the sound of a key in a lock and the sound of lock picks?"

"I do." Lanora squared her shoulders.

"You and your lock picks." Grace smiled at Lanora's reflection, stepping back. "You look perfect. You're very striking, even if your behavior is sometimes…trying. It's a shame we didn't put more effort into making you a lady."

"I am as much a lady as I care to be, thank you, and it's too late, regardless." Lanora stood. "What am I to do now, then? Go read in the parlor while I wait, and hope, that Lord William will appear at our door?" Like he didn't at the theater.

"That is exactly what you are to do, as you well know." Grace's hands rested on her hips. "Do try to restraint your mistrust."

"Mistrust is healthy." Lanora scrutinized her reflection. She smoothed her hands along her skirt. The dress was a light green. She would prefer something that matched her eyes. Pastels were insipid with her pale complexion and black hair. Even with her lack of fashion sense, she could tell a deep green would suit her better.

"If you ever do marry, you'll be permitted to wear any color you like." Grace added a knowing smile to her words.

"You must stop recognizing my every facial expression. It's practically rude." Lanora tipped her chin in the air and marched from the room.

She entered the front parlor and she took up her place in the window overlooking the front walk. She selected the spot for the light, as usual. It had nothing to do with wanting to see William the moment he appeared. After five minutes, not managing to read a single line, she set her book aside and watched the street.

He didn't arrive in his open carriage, but a larger closed one. It was magnificent. Lacquered black, with his family crest on the side. A matched team of ebony horses drew it. Lord William's coachman and tiger were dressed impeccably in Westlock grey and black.

He didn't wait for the door to be opened, but flung it outward. He stepped down, bouquet in hand, and winced as his foot met the walk. Lanora frowned, but he appeared well enough as he strode forward, resplendent in his black coat and green vest. Under the fine fabric of his outerwear and nestled against the white of his shirt and cravat, his vest was the precise shade of green she wished she could wear.

His firm knock reached the parlor. She swiveled from the window and flipped open her book. Her lips pressed into a firm line, she forced herself to take in the words so her pose of reading wouldn't be a lie. A moment later, footsteps sounded in the hall. She looked up.

He was alone, his long form framed in the doorway. No one had bothered to escort him to her. No one was there to chaperone them. Grace must have spoken to the others. They were likely all a party to her scheme of seeing Lanora wed to William.

"Lady Lanora."

At the sound of his rich, deep voice, a thrill went through her. She set aside her book. She used to think chaperones a silly thing, pointless. Now, she desperately wished for one. She wanted to talk, to hear him out and coolly evaluate his words. Left alone, she wasn't certain that would happen. In Lethbridge's office, her anger had vanished the moment his mouth met hers. It had taken all her will to call it back.

William held out the bouquet. Not London hothouse blooms. Wildflowers, from the country. Lanora felt another bit of her resolve not to be taken in slip away. She stood, and crossed the room to accept them.

"Thank you. They're lovely."

"I thought they might remind you of home."

They did. How could they not? "I should call for water."

"I think they will keep."

"Refreshments…" She forgot what words came next as he stepped into the room. He looked down at her with such intensity, she wondered if he would kiss her then and there.

"Shall we sit?" A spark of amusement glimmered in his eyes.

Amuse him, did she? Well, she was acting like a ninny, so she couldn't blame him. She nodded, moving to the couch. She lay the flowers on the table before her.

He didn't take the other side of the coach, as she expected. Instead, he settled into the chair beside her, his knee brushing hers. "Thank you for letting me call."

"Grace persuaded me I may have been rash in my judgement of you."

"Grace is a good friend. I'm lucky you have her."

He said it without a hint of reservation. Could he mean it? "She is very dear to me."

"I can see why. It's clear she has your best interests at heart."

Lanora pressed her lips closed, resisting the urge to clench her hands. Why was she so nervous? She was the wronged party, not the one who needed to win him over. "You broke into Mr. Lethbridge's office."

"And found you there." He was amused again.

Was he always so confident? "Why did you break in?"

"When you asked me, I'd already written to Darington, and heard back. He definitely requested the funds. So I investigated Mr. Finch, the foreman in charge of getting the building up. I didn't find him to be overly suspicious, so I followed the trail of money back to Lethbridge."

"You'd already written to Mr. Darington? Why not tell me so?"

"I wanted to find an answer for you first. I meant to impress you."

She flushed. "Oh." He'd broken into Mr. Lethbridge's office for her? "Picking locks is an odd skill for a future marquess."

"Is it?" He grinned, an infectious expression.

So, he didn't deny he'd picked the lock. How could he seem so honest, yet seem as if he always hid the truth from her? "You wouldn't have found anything. Well, maybe." She recalled the locked box behind the painting. "But I looked through all his files. There was nothing about Darington's home for women. Nothing from Darington at all, though I know him to be a client."

"I saw fragments of one letter. Burned. In the grate."

Lanora frowned. "How odd."

"Is that why you were there? To look for clues about the home for women?"

If he was being honest, it behooved her to be as well. "No. I followed a man who was following you. He waited outside your mistress's house. I...I wanted to confront you when you came out, but you never did, so I followed him, instead. That's when I overheard Mr. Lethbridge talking about having taken Mr. Darington's money." Should she tell him about the heiress? It hardly seemed the time.

His expression became closed. "I see."

Silence stretched between them, empty and harsh. William leaned back in his seat. Lanora's gaze dropped to the flowers on the table.

"Is she pretty?" she finally asked, feeling forlorn.

"She is, but she is not my mistress. I believe I told you that." He was guarded, his smile a memory.

"You did, but it seems very difficult to believe." How could he look at her the way he did, proclaim love for her, and yet cling to his mistress? "I assume you were with her when you didn't appear at the theater."

William ran a hand through his tousled hair, his expression closed. Meeting her eyes, he leaned forward and captured her hand. "I swear to you, she is not my mistress." His voice was low, as intense as his expression. "Who she is, that's not my secret to tell. Someone is seeking her. If she's found, she'll be in danger for her life. I shouldn't even admit to you she isn't my mistress, but I don't believe you will tell, or be believed if you did. That is all I can say of her. Please, don't press me on this."

Lanora blinked, sorting through his words. "Her life?" She hadn't expected that.

He rubbed his thumb over the back of her hand. "Do you think anything less serious would make me keep this from you? Lanora, you must believe me."

She wanted to. She longed to. Slowly, she nodded.

She could see the relief that washed over him. He smiled again, his large hand warm as it clasped hers. "A man never had so much trouble over a pretend mistress."

"You must admit, you put up a good show. The house, on that street, with someone living inside. You go there often." She grimaced. "At least, it seems that way."

"Having me followed, are you?" There was laughter in his voice. "So you do care."

"Why is Lethbridge having you followed?" Her tone was dry. "From what I overheard, he doesn't care."

"For the marquess. I told you, he requires me to be a certain sort of man. His sort. To be worthy of his holdings. To that end, he ordered Lethbridge to have me followed. My every movement is reported to him."

It seemed ridiculous. Outrageous. How could a father behave that way? Yet, it also seemed true. William's clipped words and cold tone when he spoke of his father, the shadow in his blue-green eyes. It all spoke of a terrible relationship with an awful man. "So you couldn't have courted anyone before? Not until he deemed it time?"

"I suppose I might have, though I knew he didn't wish me to wed too early. He's terribly afraid I shall fall in love with some woman and go soft."

"But won't he think you have? You took me riding. You brought me flowers."

William shook his head. "He ordered me to court you. He can't have it both ways. Besides, there is my mistress. So long as I keep that house, he won't worry I love you." His expression hardened. "I admit, if he discovers I do, he'll do all in his power to separate us."

Lanora brought her free hand to her chest, a jolt of worry going through her. "How can you think he won't discover it? I'm sure Grace has told the entire staff."

"She said they can't be bought."

"Bought? No, of course not, but they won't think it's a secret that you love me. They'll simply tell people. They're certain to be excited about it. Wouldn't you be, if someone you loved found happiness?"

He frowned. She saw him struggle with the idea.

A horrible thought came to her. "Is there anyone in your life who you love, who loves you?"

He jerked as if struck.

"I'm sorry. It was wrong of me to ask such a thing."

William shook his head, slowly. "It wasn't and yes, of course there is. There's Darington." He raised her hand to kiss. "There's you."

"And the woman in the house, who you shelter so diligently."

"Yes, and her."

Lanora felt a pang at his agreement. She wouldn't put him through the same questions again, though. She would trust his words. "The staff will already have told people. You can be sure of it."

He smiled, but the edges were brittle. "Hopefully the marquess will discount such sentiment as impossible."

"How can you live with such a father?" she whispered.

He looked away, angling a blank stare toward the wall opposite him. He swallowed, once, but his expression was empty. "You don't get to choose your father."

She reached out, lay a hand along his jaw to draw him back to her, but he didn't move. "Or your mother." Yes, her mother had died, but his had gone mad. So mad, his father sent him away. All knew the marchioness had died in the madhouse, insane. Lanora felt his jaw jump, his teeth grind together.

"I don't care to speak of my mother."

She dropped her hand. No, of course, he didn't. What was she thinking? "You say your father wishes you to marry so he may approve of your choice. Why now?"

"He's dying." There was no missing the cold glee that sparked in his eyes.

She nodded, pressing back shock. "And if you do not marry to his liking, your sister inherits his fortune?"

"Correct."

"But you want the money, so you can help people, and that would include her, yes?"

"Yes."

He was closed off now. Pain lived inside him, and she'd brought it too near the surface. He was answering her, true, and with all appearance of honesty. A wide gulf had opened between them, though. It filled her with unease. She couldn't love half a man, pretending the other half didn't exist.

"Do you care for your sister?"

He frowned. "I hardly know Madelina."

"How can that be?" She asked it before she realized it must have to do with his exile to Egypt.

"She's the daughter of my first stepmother. We lived under the same roof for three years. She was seven when the marquess sent her away. I haven't seen her once in the past nine years."

Lanora pressed her lips together. He answered her questions, but he was so cold. She'd never felt such distance between them. Not even in the moment her aunt had introduced them. He still clasped her fingers, but his grip was lax, as if he didn't recall he did so.

She pulled her hand free, bringing both up to his face this time, one on either side of his jaw. Exerting pressure, she forced him to look at her. "William, whatever happened in your life, it matters not to me. All I want to know is what sort of man you are now, today. I simply wish to understand you."

CHAPTER SEVENTEEN

To understand him? William shut his eyes, letting the warmth of her wash over him. What was he doing, dwelling in the memories Lanora inadvertently dredged up? He was permitting the marquess to ruin even this, his chance to win the woman he loved.

He opened his eyes and saw her worry. He claimed her hands in his, rubbed his thumbs over smooth skin, reveled in the softness. "And I wish for you to understand, to know me. I came today to convince you I am the man I claim to be. I didn't mean to become trapped in the past."

She offered a tentative smile. "I shouldn't have pried. It's not my place."

"It is. I want it to be." He would lay every secret bare to her, even the ones he'd already sworn not to, if he could have her by his side. "I brought these." He released her to pull out the letters. "You know Darington is my confidant. I have only his side of our conversations, but I think they will reassure you."

She shook her head. "You don't have to give them to me."

"No, but I wish to. These are only the latest few. They talk of the home for displaced women."

Her eyes dropped to the letters he proffered. She frowned. Snatching them from his hand, she brought one close, scrutinizing his address. "What is this?" She flipped it open, her eyes darting about the page. "Is this some mad game?" She looked up at him, angry.

William shook his head. He'd hardly recovered from the feelings she'd stirred, the bitter memories. Now, she was angry. He felt as if he stood in the ring, but couldn't see the opponent who kept pummeling him. "I don't understand."

Lanora held up the open letter, Darington's scrawl filling the page. "What is the meaning of this?"

"It's a letter from Darington. I believe he speaks of the home for women, and his daughter, as well as some of his latest finds. There's also an ongoing discussion on Euripides and the impact of Athenian culture on—"

"This is my father's handwriting."

William stared at her. "No, it's Darington's."

She turned the letter back around. She shook her head. "It's my father's. I would know it anywhere."

William had no idea what to make of her words. Had she gone mad?

"Wait here." She jumped up. She was out of the room, his letters still in her hand, before he grasped her intent.

He looked about, bereft. He took several slow breaths to try to calm his roiling thoughts. Sitting there alone, he finally noted the details of the parlor. Before, he could see only Lanora. Now, he took in the fine furnishings. Elegant but outdated. Not from lack of funds, that was clear. From lack of anyone caring. Long dead family members looked down from the mantel, not Lanora's mother or father.

His eyes fell on her book. Ancient Greek again. What woman read Ancient Greek?

One who'd gone mad and run off with his letters. Should he go after her? What was she playing at? Maybe this was the torment she'd devised for his imagined transgressions.

He shifted in the chair. His side throbbed. He'd suffered worse, but not many times. Cecilia had been an excruciating near half hour digging the bullet out. Not that he regretted the injury. Dodger was a good lad. William meant to see him brought up well, educated.

Where the devil was Lanora?

Rapid footsteps sounded in the hall. Though they were light, and alone, he braced himself. Only Lanora entered, bosom heaving from running. He forced his attention back to her face. This was not a time for distraction.

She perched on the edge of the sofa, crowding him, which he didn't mind. He did mind the wild look in her green eyes. She dropped a stack of letters in her lap, waving one at him.

"You see?" Her voice was as animated as the rest of her. "This? This is a letter from my father." She fluttered the letter he'd brought in her other hand. "This is your letter from Mr. Darington. What ridiculous thing have you done, William? Did you copy my father's penmanship in some bid to make false letters appear more convincing?"

Reaching out, he captured her slender wrists. "I can't see anything with you shaking them about."

"Tell me what you've done. I believe you have a good heart. I really do. I'm sure you did this out of affection."

"I haven't done anything," he said, scrutinizing the letters.

The handwriting was the same. Irrefutably so. An expert forger or…. Releasing her, he took the letters, turning them over and back. The same paper. They shared an office in Cairo. "A clerk?"

Lanora shook her head. "No, that is my father's hand. I've seen it my whole life. I can bring you old letters, from years ago."

"Could Darington dictate to your father for some reason?" But why dictate letters for so many years, and why would Lord Solworth play the role of scribe?

"You lived with him in Egypt. Don't you know if this is his handwriting?"

William dropped his gaze. Lanora was dangerously near the truth. Did he dare tell her? Moments ago, he'd vowed to, but that was before the handwriting. Now, he didn't know what to think. Good God, what if she and her father were conspiring with the marquess? But to what end?

That was the answer. The marquess. The old man would know the truth.

William folded Lord Solworth's letter. "May I borrow this? I will take it to the marquess and demand an explanation."

"That's your answer to me? That you know nothing and must leave?" Her look was incredulous.

"It is. Give me an hour. Perhaps two. I will return with the truth." All of it, if she wasn't part of this.

Lanora threw up her hands. "Do as you will, but do not fail to return with some explanation. I believe you, William. I am taking you at your word about who you are, and what you know of this." Her green eyes were luminous, beseeching. "Please don't break my trust."

The need to kiss her was nearly insurmountable, as if this might be his final chance. Refusing to believe that, he tucked the letters into his coat and stood. "By your leave." With a nod, he left.

William strode from the townhouse, wincing as he jogged down the steps. "Take me to the old man," he ordered his driver, and climbed into the carriage. It wasn't until he set out that he realized he'd left the bulk of Darington's letters behind.

Hooves clattered on cobblestone. William winced with each bounce. He hadn't told his man to hurry. Evidently, his attitude had been enough.

They reached the old man's townhouse in record time. William took the steps at a quick pace, giving the butler the barest nod as he shouldered open the door and hurried by. To his surprise, footsteps sounded behind him.

"My lord."

The butler never spoke without being addressed. William halted, turned.

"My lord, the marquess is not in his office."

"He's not?" William pulled out his watch. The old man was always in his office at this time of day.

"He's above stairs. In bed."

William tucked the watch away. He eyed the staircase. He hadn't entered the private areas of the house in nearly a decade. "I see."

Steeling himself, he went up. To reach the marquess's room, he must walk past his own, Charles's, and the room where three marchionesses, including his mother, had suffered at the hands of the marquess. Jaw clenched, William made the march. Unlike Cecilia's home, where the walls were blessedly bare, here they were lined with ancestors. Grim eyes followed William down the hall.

The old man was indeed abed. He lay propped on pillows, shadowed in the vast canopied bed. The only light was his eyes, glinting evilly in the dark.

William strode across the room and yanked open the curtains to let in light. The window followed, for a fetid smell lurked in the perfume-soaked air.

"You heard I was dying and came to gloat." The voice was wheezing, thin.

"I did not. I should rather never have laid eyes on you again." Bracing himself, Willian went to the bedside.

The old man smiled, his skin stretched thin and translucent. "That's my boy. I have made you over well. No sentiment to weaken you."

"Not where you're concerned, old man."

"Not anywhere. Even gave up your mistress, when she made a fuss over you marrying. Good lad."

William shook his head. Yes, that's the conclusion the marquess would come to. He'd known as much when he wrote to Lethbridge about it.

A skeletal hand reached out, plucking at the bedcovers. "Can't marry Solworth's chit, though. I forbid it. They say you love her. Love is weakness, boy. When will you learn? You never learn."

"I will marry whomever I please."

"You won't. I sent Lethbridge to get the will. I want your word you won't marry the chit or I'll sign it. No heir of mine is marrying for love."

"That's odd, because I am your heir and I shall." He enjoyed the fury that sparked in the old man's eyes. "Sign a new will if you like, if you've the strength left. It matters little to me."

The marquess attempted a wheezing, unintelligible protest, which William didn't bother to decipher. Lethbridge may very well have designs on Madelina, as Cecilia suspected, but Lethbridge was going to jail. William would find enough evidence against him. Madelina would become William's ward, and he would protect her. Nor would his goal of bettering the poorest parts of London suffer. Lanora would have all the funds they required to aid the poor. It was clear to him now that she would be an ally in the task.

William stared with loathing at the form lying in the bed. There was only one thing he required from the marquess. Not his fortune. Not his approval. Only an answer. He pulled the letters from his coat.

"What is the meaning of this?"

The marquess coughed. Blood flecked his lips. "They're letters, boy."

"One of them is from Lord Solworth to his daughter, the other from Mr. Darington to me. Why are they in the same hand?"

The marquess's cackling laugh ended in another fit of coughing. He fell back, eyes closed.

William watched him breathe, jaw clenched. He folded the letters and put them away. Reaching out, he shook the old man by his boney shoulders. "I asked you a question."

Dark eyes flickered open. Old yellowed teeth, blood tinged, grinned at him. "Shaking a dying man? That's my boy."

William resisted the urge to shake him harder. He pulled his hands away and dusted them on his pants, as if he'd touched something foul. "Answer me."

"They are the same. There is no Darington. Solworth invented him."

William took a half step back, stunned. Darington had exploits. Adventures. He was reported about in the paper and co-wrote learned articles with Lord Solworth. William and Darington had corresponded since William was fourteen. "How? Why?"

"His wife died. He wished to escape. Love makes a man weak."

That part of the story William knew. "What has that to do with you, or me?"

The marquess drew in several wheezing breaths. "Solworth had no money. His father wouldn't fund Egypt. He'd only begot the girl, after all. I needed an excuse for your absence, your ill manners."

William stared at the gasping form on the bed. "You funded Solworth, not Darington. You paid for his first expedition in exchange for him inventing an alibi for my years with Mother."

The marquess cackled again, gleeful. "You look up to him, and it's a lie. Twelve years of lies. I prayed I would live to see the look on your face when you found out."

The old man's laughter turned into another coughing fit. He gasped for air. Blood red spittle ran down his chin. His face began to turn purple. His eyes flew wide. William stayed where he was, making no effort to help, though he didn't know how one would. The marquess stilled. Silence fell. The body on the bed moved no more, would never stir again.

William closed his eyes for a long moment, then drew in a slow breath and strode from the room. He didn't bother to close the door. He went downstairs, out of that place, and into his carriage. His coachman came to the window.

"Where to, my lord?"

"Back to Solworth House. No need to hurry."

His words sounded far away. He must have looked a sight, for his coachman eyed him a long moment before he nodded and disappeared. The carriage dipped, then started forward.

William took out the letters, dimly seen in the interior of the carriage. A lie. Twelve years of lies.

No. He shook his head. He couldn't believe that. The name, yes. The existence of his confidant, yes. Lies. The words, never. William was not so poor a judge of other men as that. Darington's...that was, Solworth's words were real. One need simply change out the name and the remainder was real.

And Lady Lanora was Darington's daughter. Lanora was the free, kind, caring creature he'd grown up reading about. That's why the letters never named her, why all attempts at finding Mr. Darington's daughter had failed. It was Lanora. It had always been her.

Lightness filled him. He wasn't giving up the dream of Darington's daughter by falling in love with Lanora. He was realizing it. Was it any wonder he was more drawn to her every day? He'd already loved her for years.

The carriage came to a stop. William stuffed the letters back in his coat. He jumped down from the carriage, forgetting his stitches in his joy to see Lanora, to tell her all.

Before he could take the steps, the door flew open. Grace ran out. He grabbed her by the shoulders as she all but fell down the steps, steadying her.

"My lord, thank Heaven you've come," Grace cried. "She's gone off to that evil attorney. She said she must know the truth. I couldn't stop her."

CHAPTER EIGHTEEN

Lanora hurried up the steps to Lethbridge's office. She believed William would return with answers. She truly did. She could not wait, though. She would not sit wringing her hands and fretting, waiting on another to do for her what she could do herself. The attorney would know what transpired, and she would get it from him, or his lockbox. Whichever proved easier.

The outer door stood open, but the one at the top of the steps was closed, locked. She pressed her lips together. She'd come prepared this time. She carried her lock picks and a pistol in her reticule.

Lanora looked down the steps. The open outer door suggested Lethbridge and his clerk weren't done for the day. She had no way to know when they might return.

She set to work on the door. If the worst came to pass, she would simply hide, as she had before. At least this time she'd be able to escape if she got locked in.

It was a simple lock. She slipped inside and closed the door. With enough light, and knowing what she sought, it took only a moment to get down the strongbox. She set it on Lethbridge's desk. Opening it was trickier, for the lock was better than the one on the door, but not insurmountable.

After long moments, tension coiling tight in her gut, the lock gave way with an audible click. Inside were two documents. Both appeared to be wills. Lanora set them side by side, reading. They belonged to the Marquess of Westlock, William's father. He'd been telling the truth.

Further examination showed the signed document left everything to William. Oddly, there was a section specifying that nothing of any sort was to be left to his stepmother, Lady Cecilia, the marquess's third wife. Lanora frowned. If Lady Cecilia was of ill health and residing on the Mediterranean, why cut her from his will? The old marquess had also left only a small sum for his daughter, Lady Madelina.

Lanora picked up the other document. She could see it also went to lengths to make it clear that Lady Cecilia was to have nothing. Aside from that, the remainder was very different from the signed document. Everything that wasn't entailed went to Lady Madelina, a girl of sixteen.

Lanora frowned. A girl of sixteen. She flipped to the last page. It specified that Lethbridge was to be the girl's sole guardian and have complete control over her assets.

"It's Lady Madelina he intends to marry," she whispered.

"And marry the girl, I shall."

Lanora spun.

A thin, balding man stood in the doorway, pistol pointed at her. "Lady Lanora. How good of you to call."

"Mr. Lethbridge." She clutched her reticule in one hand. Was there any means of freeing her pistol that wouldn't rouse suspicion?

"This is very inconvenient of you. I was just on my way to have that signed, which will render you irrelevant."

Lanora's gaze went to the document in question, then back to the pistol. "Then I don't matter now."

"Ah, but you do. I heard what you said." Lethbridge frowned. "Where you came by the notion I don't know, but I can't have you spreading that about."

Could she distract him, perhaps engage him well enough he wouldn't notice if she drew her pistol? She wouldn't have believed he would shoot, but he had the weapon cocked and she'd heard his cold-blooded words the night she was locked in.

"What do you mean, you're on your way to have the second will signed?"

He grinned, showing uneven teeth. "Not finding Lord William as attractive without his fortune? I can't say I blame you. The man's a wastrel."

Anger shot through her. "I daresay he's a better man than you, Mr. Lethbridge."

"What's this?" Lethbridge's gaze narrowed. "Don't tell me you actually care for Greydrake? A more useless bounder can hardly be found in the whole of England. I took you for more intelligent than that."

"I will not stand here and be insulted," Lanora said at her coldest. "I suggest you claim your document and leave, sir. I believe your master is in ill health. You wouldn't wish him to expire while you're away."

He cringed. Lanora dared to hope her tone worked. Lethbridge would be accustomed to obeying officious lords and ladies. His gaze touched on the pistol he held. He smiled and stood straighter.

"Greydrake is so disreputable, in fact, the world might blame him if the woman he's courting vanishes," Lethbridge muttered. He shook his head and focused on her. "I'm not certain what to do with you, Lady Lanora. Until I decide, I'm afraid you'll have to stay in there." He gestured toward the door of the small records room.

Lanora could free herself as soon as he left, but what about William's inheritance, and his poor sister? She couldn't let Lethbridge hold guardianship over an innocent young girl. It was unthinkable. She had to stop him from taking the will to the marquess. Unsigned, it was meaningless.

"Why has the marquess agreed to sign this?" She tapped the pages. With her other hand, she carefully worked at the closure on her reticule, but it was fastened tight. "Am I not a suitable bride?" She lifted her chin, as if insulted.

He looked her up and down, his gaze speculative. "I'm sure you'd be a wonderful bride. A bit headstrong, but that can be beaten out of you. Sole heir to a fortune, as well. Rest assured, it's not your qualities."

"Why then?" she pressed, actually curious now. She was on William's list of choices, not that she'd admit knowledge of the page to Lethbridge. Had word already reached the marquess that William said he loved her, as she feared it would?

"As I said, nothing to do with you. I need Greydrake to fail. I was delighted when he settled on you. I knew he would. You're the perfect choice to aggravate the marquess. I thought the task of winning you insurmountable, but somehow, he wormed his way into your good graces." He grimaced. "I had to convince the marquess that Greydrake is in love with you. No small task, for his lordship doesn't believe in the sentiment. If I'd any notion you would be so easily wooed, I wouldn't have made you an option."

"An option?" she asked, playing for time as she worked at the stubborn clasp. "What does that mean?"

He flicked a hand toward the record room, where she'd found the page. "I created a list of suitable options. Women the marquess would approve of, but who weren't likely to accept Greydrake. Then, I thought you never would. He must have charms not obvious to a gentleman like myself."

Lanora resisted the urge to say she saw no gentleman before her. "He chose me from a list?" She worked to dredge up the outrage she'd initially felt. If she could convince Lethbridge she didn't care about William, would he let her go? She took in the way he kept looking her over, like a Christmas goose. Could she convince him she would marry him? If he would put down the pistol, she would have hers out.

"Didn't mention that little bit, did he? I told you he's a cad. If you didn't suffer from a feeble female mind, you would have seen as much for yourself."

Lanora pressed her lips together in an effort to contain her anger. He was pointing a pistol at her, after all. It was hardly the time to express her feelings on the idea that she, or any female, suffered in any way as a result of possessing a woman's mind.

"Do you mean he used me?" she demanded, helping Lethbridge come to the point.

"Of course. As he uses all women." He grinned. "He keeps a mistress, you know. Not just one. A series of them. One after the other, as he grows bored. Just turned one out the other day. Apparently, she kept him occupied for nearly two days, after learning he's courting you. Likely, trying to secure his affections. All she did was bore him." His smile turned malicious. "As you will, if you wed him. As you're boring me now. Get in the record room." He took a step forward, menacing.

"Wait. You must tell me something first," she cried, desperate to stall for time, to find a way to retrieve her firearm and turn the table on the hideous man.

"You're in no position to make demands of me, my lady."

"It's about Mr. Darington. You represent him, don't you?"

He frowned. "What about Mr. Darington?"

Lanora opened her mouth, but no words came out. She didn't wish to ask about the handwriting. She was loath to give this man any information he didn't have.

"Well?" He punctuated the word with a wave of the pistol.

Nor should she bring up the money Lethbridge had stolen. Not while his aggravation increased. She must say something, though, and soon, if his look was any indication. "He's Lord William's mentor."

"Perhaps."

That was an odd reply. "He works with my father, in Egypt."

"The world knows that."

"I've never met him, and he raised Lord William."

Lethbridge scowled.

She was losing his interest. "I want to know more about Mr. Darington, outside what's in the papers. That's why I came here, to ask about him."

His gaze slid around the room, pausing on the opening above the mantel. The painting that should cover it leaned against the wall beside the fireplace.

His roving gaze dropped to the open strongbox. "How did you get into that? How did you even enter this office? I sent my clerk home and locked the door."

Now she wished she'd let him lock her away already. "The door was open. I came in and called out, but no one was here."

His eyes narrowed, bright with suspicion. "And the strongbox? How did you get the wills out, or know where to find them?" He moved a step nearer.

"I didn't." She tried to back away, but the desk halted her retreat. "How could I? I came in to look for you and found them." She swallowed, not feigning nervousness. "I shouldn't have read them, I know. I let my curiosity get the better of me."

"And the girl? You said I plan to wed her. You knew." Anger sparked in his eyes.

"No." She shook her head. "I mean, I said it, I did, but I didn't know before I read the will."

He glanced at the document, as if it might reveal something. "It doesn't say I'm to marry her."

"It says you will be her guardian. I was guessing. It was only a supposition."

He watched her for a long moment, pistol an arm's length from her chest. At that range, there was no chance he would miss. Could she count on it jamming? Not something she wished to bet her life on.

He gestured with the pistol. "Get in the record room before I decide I must shoot you."

"Yes, of course." She clutched her arms close, trying to make clinging to her reticule look natural. She did her best to appear vanquished, cowed. She still meant to prevent him from getting the will signed. How, she didn't know, but she would come up with a plan. One that didn't involve being shot.

He took another step. She could smell his breath now, onion and mead. Lanora slid along the desk toward the doorway to the little room. She tried not to look at the will. There was nothing she could do. Once she was free of him, perhaps, but not now. She backed into the little room.

Lethbridge closed the door. The key turned in the lock. Lanora slumped against the cluttered shelves in relief, happy to have the stout wood between her and Lethbridge. She'd never had a pistol pointed at her before. It was an altogether unpleasant experience.

She went to the door and put her ear to it. She could hear him moving. From the sound of it, he was replacing the strongbox and painting. She should have thrown the second will on the fire. She wouldn't have had time to stir the flames, but a slightly scorched, charcoal-covered document wouldn't look respectable enough to convince anyone it was meant. She nearly cursed, angry she hadn't thought of tossing the pages in the fireplace until she was locked away.

As soon as he was gone, she would free herself. She would go to the militia and tell them everything. Maybe, on her word, they would lock Lethbridge away. Hers was only the word of a woman, not so highly counted in a court of law, but she was daughter to a duke. At least she could try. Lethbridge would have a difficult time marrying Lady Madelina from prison.

She heard him cross back to his desk. There was a rustle, then the sound of pages being tapped into a neat stack. He was leaving with the will.

"Lethbridge, you bastard," a familiar voice roared, footsteps bursting into the office. "Where is she?"

CHAPTER NINETEEN

William came to a skidding halt in the doorway, fists clenched, glaring at the attorney's back. Lethbridge stood before his desk. Lanora wasn't in the room. Her carriage waited out front, though. Her coachman said she'd entered. The only other way out was through Lethbridge's window. The curtains were pulled tight. No breeze stirred them.

"Lord William. I should have expected you." Lethbridge set a neat stack of papers on the desk, beside another. He turned, brandishing a pistol.

"I asked you a question," William snarled. "What have you done with her?"

"You seem to think I won't use this." Hatred glinted in Lethbridge's eyes. "You nobles. You think yourselves untouchable."

"Oh, I think you'll use it. Never fear." William kept his voice low, menacing. "I just don't think one shot will stop me from throttling the life out of you. Tell me where she is."

Lethbridge paled, hand shaking slightly. "She's not here, or are you blind as well as stupid?"

"She came in. No one saw her leave." William looked to the only other door, leading to the small room where Lethbridge kept his records. Was the knob moving?

"She's not here. What right have you to barge into my office? I have business to attend to. I will be on my way."

"What sort of business, Lethbridge?"

"None of your concern. Something for your father." He looked at the pistol in his hand, seeming confused. "I will use this if you continue to behave in so violent a manner. Don't think I won't."

"We established that." William folded his arms across his chest. "And you can take a seat. You have no business with the marquess."

Lethbridge shook the pistol at William, as if the gesture could increase its intimidation. "My business is mine, and the marquess's. You have no say in it."

"No, I don't, but neither does he." A hard grin curved William's lips. "The marquess is dead."

Lethbridge staggered back against the desk, pistol dipping. "No."

"I assure you, he is. I just came from his townhouse, where I had the distinct pleasure of watching him breathe his last." William stepped into the room, reaching for the weapon. "The game is up."

"No." Lethbridge scrambled around behind his desk, trying to keep the pistol aimed at William.

William winced as the attorney nearly tripped on his chair. The man was dangerous with a firearm. He had it cocked. He might shoot by mistake.

Reaching across his desk, Lethbridge pulled one of the stacks of pages to him. "I will sign it. It will be your word to mine that he didn't. He could hardly grip a pen of late. Any scribble will do." With his free hand, he started fumbling at his desk drawer, where he kept fresh pens.

"Yes. Your word against mine, and who do you think will be believed?"

Lethbridge went still. He looked up, his expression feral. "They'll believe me when you're dead and Madelina is mine, along with the marquess's fortune."

The man was moments from madness. William would not let him slide over the edge before he found out where Lanora was. "Is that how you plan to repay the money you stole from Darington? With the marquess's fortune? When you drew up that list, you planned all along for me to fail."

"Of course I did," Lethbridge cried. He gestured wildly with the pistol. "What respectable woman would marry you? How was I to know Lady Lanora is England's greatest fool?"

He had to calm Lethbridge down before he really did shoot, though he was as like to hit himself as William. "Why take the money? I would have guessed you make a good living."

"Toadying to the likes of you? Is that what you call good?"

"I've never been easy to deal with." William tried to control the anger in his tone. Was she in the record room? If so, why didn't she call out? But where else could Lethbridge have spirited her off to?

"Not easy? You're the worst sort of degenerate. You spend more on each of your mistresses than I make in a year, and all for women you discard on a whim."

"Once I marry Lady Lanora, I won't keep a mistress any longer. You won't need to worry about the sums." Or freedom.

"Not keep a mistress? A man like you?" Lethbridge looked baffled. "You told me you would never be foolish enough to love a wife."

"I lied. I told you what I knew the marquess wanted to hear. You know how he was." William attempted a smile. "You'll find me a much more reasonable man now, and he won't trouble you with his demands. You and I, we'll work something out with the money you borrowed. Darington will understand."

Lethbridge's hand began to shake again.

"Better yet, we won't tell Darington," William hurried on. "I'll cover the debt."

Narrow, suspicious eyes regarded him over the pistol.

"What did you need the money for? Perhaps I can cover that as well," William added, his voice the calmest he could muster.

"I invested in trade. A storm sank the fleet."

"That's rough luck," William said. "We've all been there. I understand." Would the man ever put down the pistol? To Lethbridge's left, the door to the record room inched open. William caught a flicker of pale green fabric and silken limbs.

Lethbridge shook his head. "Why should I settle for some when I can have all?"

Arm holding the pistol bobbing and shaking, but generally pointed toward William, Lethbridge eased open the drawer he'd fumbled with earlier. He pulled out a fresh pen. His eyes dropped to the closed inkpot. He frowned. He leaned across the desk, arranging pen, ink and one of the stacks of papers on the left edge.

The door to the record room inched wider. Relief assailed William as he recognized Lanora. Shock followed hard behind. She held a pistol, pointed toward Lethbridge.

"You will have to sign it," Lethbridge said. "I can't open the ink." He shook the pistol again for emphasis.

William wanted to roar in frustration. Did either of them realize how deadly the weapons they held were? What mad reality had he stepped into? He should have brought a pistol of his own, so he could put an end to this.

"Sign what?" William asked as calmly as he could manage. He didn't dare look full at Lanora, or he'd give her away. What she planned to do, he had no idea.

"The unsigned will. The one leaving Madelina everything, and giving her into my care. Sign as your father. Try to make it convincing. Your life depends on it."

William started toward the desk. Lethbridge was a fool. This was William's chance. The desk wasn't that wide. When he reached for the inkwell, Lethbridge was his.

"Don't sign it," Lanora cried, leaping from behind the door, pistol at the ready.

Lethbridge jumped. He swung toward Lanora. William lunged across the remaining distance to the desk, ignoring the pain in his side. Quicker than William would have credited, Lethbridge turned back.

"Get back," he squawked.

William went still. The pistol was just out of arm's reach, pointed at his face.

"Lower your pistol, Mr. Lethbridge, or I'll shoot you," Lanora ordered.

"Lower yours or I'll shoot him," Lethbridge countered without taking his eyes from William.

"For God's sake," William growled. If this kept up, someone was going to get hurt. Now that he was sure Lanora was safe, he didn't give a damn about Lethbridge, but there was every chance that, once bullets began flying, Lanora could be injured.

A slow smile spread across Lethbridge's face. "I propose you shoot Lord William, my lady."

"Don't be ridiculous," she said.

"A lover's spat. Not that anyone will know. You shoot him, and it will be our secret." Lethbridge's words dripped oil.

"I will not shoot him, but I will shoot you if you don't put that pistol down."

William took some satisfaction in the certainty of her tone.

"I think you will shoot him, when you learn how he's deceived you."

"I know about the list. I know about his mistress. We have no secrets."

Now, Lanora's sureness knifed into William's heart. Lethbridge was alive with glee. William's pulse raced. What did the attorney know?

"Then you must also know that Lord William never lived in Egypt with Mr. Darington. He lived on the poorest streets in London, as a beggar. He and his whore of a mother. She didn't go mad, she ran off, and took him with her."

Air hissed through William's teeth. "Call my mother a whore again and it will be your last word, Lethbridge."

"William," Lanora asked, stunned, "is it true?"

William didn't look at her.

Lethbridge smirked.

Red anger made the edges of William's vision fuzzy, but he could see the attorney with clarity. "How long have you known? The marquess would never have told you."

"She told me. When she lay dying in that cell. I pretended I was there to help her and she told me everything. About your brother, the life you'd been leading. How you begged for bread. Everything. I've spent years kowtowing to you, a man hardly better than street scum."

"William." Lanora's voice was soft.

He couldn't look at her. He had to focus on Lethbridge, his enemy. More than that, he feared Lanora's expression. There would be pity there, if he was lucky. More likely, disgust. It was one thing to hand out bread and treat her gentrified staff as human. It was another to have kissed a man who'd lived in the squalor of London, begging for his food.

"Shoot him, Lady Lanora," Lethbridge urged. "Set yourself free of this lying scum."

"It all makes sense," Lanora said, her incredulous tone finally drawing his gaze. "William, you're—" She broke off, looking from Lethbridge back to him. "It all makes sense now."

Was that respect in her voice? Now that William looked, he couldn't read her face.

"Yes, now you know." Lethbridge was triumphant. "He was about to trick you into marrying him, a man unfit for the daughter of a duke. No one will blame you for killing him."

"Do you know what I think, Mr. Lethbridge?" Lanora said, her voice firm, strident. "It's not having to work for Lord William that embitters you. It's knowing that you, no matter what path you take in life, will never be his equal. No amount of fortune or education will ever make you half the man he is. Not even half the man he was as a boy raised on the streets of London. And you can't live with that."

Lethbridge turned on her, eyes wild with rage. William lunged forward, dove across the desk. He crashed into Lethbridge. A pistol fired. They slammed into Lethbridge's chair, the wall, the floor. Coming up on his knees, William grabbed Lethbridge by the collar. His fist smashed into the attorney's face. Bright blood sprayed from Lethbridge's nose.

William released the torn fabric. Lethbridge's head dropped to the floor, bouncing once beside the shattered inkwell. William stood. Pain lanced through his side. He winced, pressing his hand to the gunshot wound to find fresh blood. His leap over the desk must have torn his stitches.

He prodded Lethbridge with his boot. The man was out cold. Nearby, the pistol lay spent. A glance upward showed the bullet lodged in the ceiling. Finally, reluctant in spite of her speech, he turned to Lanora.

She still held a gun, pointed right at him.

CHAPTER TWENTY

Lanora stood motionless, stunned. William stood over Lethbridge's unconscious form, masculine perfection. Tousled curls, coat askew. She'd never seen anything like his dive across the desk. The way he grabbed Lethbridge, the punch, it was all so...thrilling.

She'd been scared in the moment. Terrified, really, that William would be shot. When the pistol fired, she'd stifled a scream.

Now, safe, she felt wholly different. She uncocked the pistol she held and tossed it behind her into the record room, where her reticule remained. Turning back, she saw William's expression of relief.

Lanora frowned. "You didn't imagine I would shoot you?"

"You were pointing a pistol at me."

"Are you that sort of gentleman, then, who doesn't listen to a word a lady says?"

A grin tugged at the corner of his mouth. "Only when she's directing a deadly weapon my way."

"That, my lord, is the time you must listen to her most."

"True enough." He stepped over Lethbridge, wincing.

Lanora hurried to him, her eyes on the hand he pressed to his left side. She pulled at it, seeing blood. A gasp escaped her. "You're hurt. I didn't think he hit you."

"He didn't. It's nothing."

"It's not nothing. You're bleeding." She yanked on his arm, dragging him toward the leather couch. "Come, sit. Will he wake soon?"

William chuckled, the sound only slightly strained, and let her lead him.

"Does your amusement mean he'll sleep?"

"He won't wake soon," William said.

"You're sure?"

"I've hit enough men to know." He'd reached the couch, but didn't sit. "Collect your things. I'll send my tiger for the militia. You shouldn't be here when they come, or have your name dragged into this. Your man can take you home."

Was he mad? "Absolutely not. You need a surgeon, and I am not leaving your side."

He shook his head. "A doctor will have questions, and might talk. I have somewhere to go, someone who will see to me, and you must go home."

"But why worry over questions? We've done nothing wrong." She scrutinized his face. "What aren't you telling me? Why can't I go with you?"

His look softened. "Do you truly wish to?" He gestured at the room, papers scattered everywhere. Lethbridge's feet sticking out from under the desk. "This can be covered up, explained away. Once you get in my carriage with me, you will be compromised. That's not how I want to make you mine, Lanora. I would have you agree to marry me, not be forced to."

She stared up into his warm hazel eyes. "Did you ask me to marry you, just now?"

"I've been trying to get you to marry me since we met. All in all, I think I'm doing a splendid job."

"Do you?" The nerve of him, so certain, and tall, handsome… She suppressed a sigh.

"Are you going to come with me or take your carriage home?" The intensity in his tone belied the simplicity of the question.

"I'm coming with you." For some reason, the words came out breathless.

"I love you too," he said, dropping a kiss on her forehead.

Lanora gaped at him.

He reached out and used a gentle finger to close her mouth. "Collect your things."

She nodded, feeling somewhat dizzy as she crossed the room and gathered up her pistol and reticule. She turned back to find William tossing a stack of papers into the fireplace.

"The unsigned will," he said. "It's the one that didn't get knocked from the desk, of course."

She frowned. "That's because he put it to the left." Her frown deepened as she studied the desk. "You must have only just got the inkwell. The pen didn't move. Shall I gather the other?"

William stirred up the fire. The pages caught, momentarily brightening the room with new flame. "Whoever cleans this up can gather them." He turned from the fire. "That should be good enough. We should go."

Lanora nodded. It was more important to get William to, well, wherever they were going than to pick up the pages of the marquess's will.

She followed him across the clerk's office and down the steps, aware he was moving more slowly than usual. When they reached the landing, he drew his hand from his injured side and wiped it clean on a kerchief. He quickly ran a hand though his hair, restoring it to its usual controlled disorder. He drew out gloves and pulled them on, covering the knuckles of his left hand, reddened from colliding with Lethbridge's face. Lastly, he tugged his coat to order and fluffed his cravat. She realized, his coat being black, only close scrutiny would reveal he was injured. He turned to her, looked her up and down, and nodded.

"Will you send your driver home and then join me in my carriage?" he asked, his tone perfectly urbane, as if he wasn't injured, and as if he hadn't, moments ago, broken a man's nose.

Lanora nodded. He opened the door for her. Two splendid carriages, one with the crest of his house and one with hers, stood without. Lanora hurried out to reassure her coachman she was well, and sent him home to give Grace the same news. She also informed him that, though it was pending her father's blessing, she and Lord William were engaged.

She felt a bit bad as she climbed into William's carriage, handed up by an expressionless servant. She'd used her coachman's relief that she was well, and joy at her engagement, to send him away before he realized she wasn't going with him. She hoped he wouldn't be too upset.

It was dark inside William's carriage, for he had the curtains drawn. She settled into the seat across from him. He knocked on the roof and they set out.

"Where are we going, if not to a surgeon?" She kept her voice low. "Am I to assume your men are not to know you're injured?"

"That is a safe assumption. You will not care for where we're going, and undoubtedly there will be rumors sparked, but please wait until we're inside before questioning me. I will explain."

Lanora mulled that over while they rode. She wished to ask him about his mother, and his brother. What Lethbridge had meant when he said he knew all. Even in the dim interior, she could see the strain on William's features, the pain etched there. She kept her lips pressed tight over her questions.

She couldn't keep the shock from her face when she was handed down from the carriage. She was quite familiar with the street. Not long ago, she'd spent hours staring at it. They'd arrived at William's mistress's townhouse. She shot him an incredulous glance. He replied with a slight shake of his head.

He led the way up the steps and knocked. After a moment, the door swung inward. William ushered her inside. To compound the strangeness, the boy who'd accepted bread from her was there. He was clean, and dressed in new clothes, but she couldn't fail to recognize him.

"No new servants yet?" William asked the boy while tugging off his gloves.

"No, your lordship."

"Good. That simplifies things."

The boy darted a look at Lanora, then turned back to William. "You gone and done yourself harm again, haven't you? Her ladyship is going to be right angry."

"Yes, well, I second her complaint." Tossing his gloves toward a table, William pressed his hand to his side. "I'll go to my room. If you could tell her I require her services?"

He required what? Lanora stared at him.

The boy nodded his chin at her. "Why's Mrs. Smith dressed like a lady?"

"Because Mrs. Smith is really Lady Lanora." He offered Lanora a smile tight with pain. Sweat stood out on his forehead. "This is Dodger."

"Lady Lanora?" Dodger's eyes were wide. "So she's the one you're wanting to marry?"

"She is. Now, go get the lady of the house and please, help her with whatever she asks. I'm afraid I've pulled my stitches."

"Yes, your lordship." The boy scurried off.

He was sending for his mistress? He required her services? Lanora drew in a breath and reminded herself that she trusted William. He had an excellent explanation. She was sure of it. She was also sure she'd better hear it soon.

"Would it be impertinent of me to ask you to walk beside me up the steps?" William asked.

"Do you need to lean on me?" She moved to his side, worry for him driving back suspicion.

"No, I can manage. Your presence alone will bolster my spirit." He offered a grimace that was likely meant to be a smile. "Rather, the desire not to fall down the stairs while you watch will bolster my resolve. I don't want to ruin the image of masculine strength I've cultivated."

They made their way up the steps and down the hall, where William let them into a room that was neat, modish and clearly his. It even smelled like him, shaving soap, clean linens and masculinity. He settled on the edge of the bed. A woman burst through the adjoining door.

Petite, blonde, with an almost unearthly beauty, she looked to be perhaps four years Lanora's senior. She stopped when she saw them. Her lips broke into a wide smile. She rushed forward and embraced Lanora.

"Welcome." She stepped back. "I am so happy to meet you. You have no notion how much so. You're the first friend I've had in years." For all the brightness of her smile, tears stood in her luminous blue eyes.

"Lanora, this is Lady Cecilia Greydrake, my stepmother."

"Your…" Lanora took the woman in again, with new eyes. "You're not in the Mediterranean."

"Heavens, no. Didn't he tell you?" She raised a hand to her mouth. "He brought you up here without telling you who I am?"

"He promised he had a good explanation," Lanora said, dazed by the revelation. He hadn't lied.

Lady Cecilia's smile would brighten even the dreariest winter day. "And you believed him? Oh, how wonderful." She looked as if she might shed more tears. "Still, William, how could you—" She broke off as she turned to him. He was pale, his gaze slightly unfocused. "Oh. I see. Not quite yourself."

Cecilia's tone remained bright, but Lanora saw worry in her face, the tension that sprang up around her mouth.

"He said you could help him," Lanora said.

"Yes, likely. I'm good with this sort of thing. I've had a lot of time to read, and learn, and plenty of practice on him." Her worry remained. "I'll go set Dodger to boiling more water. We'll need lots of clean linen."

"How can I help?"

"Get his clothes off, for a start."

Lanora's face filled with heat.

"Oh dear. I apologize. I only mean off the top half of him." Lady Cecilia patted her on the arm. "Will that do? I mean, you'll be all right baring him to the waist?"

"I'll offer her encouragement." William's voice was amused, but his words strained at the edges.

"He's losing blood. I need to get my things. I'll stitch him up, but this is the second time. He'll run out of skin. You must make sure he stays in bed for at least two weeks this time. Longer, if you can manage it."

"Yes, of course." Lanora had no notion how, but she would make sure he healed. This time.

Lady Cecilia gave her an encouraging smile, another pat on the arm.

"Cecilia." They both turned toward William. "He's dead."

"Dead?" The small blonde woman swayed.

Lanora put an arm about her, worried she would topple.

"He's really dead?" Lady Cecilia whispered.

"He's really dead."

Tears filled Lady Cecilia's eyes. She blinked, sending them skittering down her cheeks. A huge smile lit her face. "Finally," she said, the word full of a ferocious joy. She gave Lanora a fierce hug and hurried from the room.

Yet another thing in need of explanation, but one look assured Lanora now was not the time for lengthy talks, especially on delicate matters. She moved to stand before William, and steeled herself to do as Lady Cecilia asked.

"I suppose we must start with your coat."

"Excellent plan. I knew you had a good head on your shoulders." He smiled at her, though the expression looked pained.

Lanora eased off his coat. Not sure what to do with it, she folded it, bloody side up, and set it on the floor. She hoped it wouldn't ruin anything. Next, she unbuttoned his green vest, left side streaked with blood. Sight of the blood sent panic through her. How badly was he injured? She pressed her lips into a firm line, worried for him.

Still, with each button on the vest, her face grew hotter. His cravat provided the distraction of a complex knot, but once it was removed and she was confronted with his shirt laces, her heart took up such a rapid beat, she thought she might faint. She couldn't sort out her emotions. Fear for him was strong, but something else, as well. Something unfamiliar, frightening in its own right.

She reached for the laces with hands that shook.

William caught her wrists. "Cut it off."

Lanora stared at him, confused.

"Use my shaving razor and cut the shirt off. I'll never get it over my head."

"Oh."

She collected the blade and returned to the bed. She couldn't cut the front. It would be...she couldn't. To cut the back, she must climb onto the bed behind him. With a deep breath, she said a prayer she wouldn't cut him or her shaking hands in the process and climbed onto the mattress.

By the time she had his shirt off, revealing his bandaged-wrapped middle, Lanora shook all over. She felt as if she'd run a mile, uphill the whole way. She put the tattered shirt with his other garments. Her palms tingled, the memory of each time they'd brushed across his warm skin emblazoned on them. She tried not to look, even while she worked, but visions of his muscled back and sculpted chest were scorched in her mind.

Lady Cecilia bustled into the room, followed by a burdened Dodger. The little blonde woman made a sound of dismay. "What have you done to yourself, William? Dodger, put that clean sheet down beside him. No, leave it folded. Perhaps we can save the bedclothes this time. William, lay down."

Lanora drew back, taking deep breaths. She let Lady Cecilia's bright efficiency fill the room, a buffer between her and William. Legs unsteady, she settled into a chair. Trying not to be jealous, which would be foolish in the extreme, she watched Lady Cecilia tend William.

CHAPTER TWENTY-ONE

William woke to a room lit by moonlight. He drew in a deep breath, aware each of his new stitches, but less pain. An apparition rose from the chair near the open window and glided toward the bed.

"You're awake," Lanora said. She lay a cool hand on his forehead. "You don't feel warm. Lady Cecilia said I must wake her if you have a fever."

William caught her hand and caressed her soft skin with his thumb. "I'm well. I'm strong."

"Fortunately." She perched on the edge of the bed "What were you thinking, jumping over a desk with a bullet wound in your side?"

"I was thinking that Lethbridge might be fool enough to take you from me and I would do anything to prevent that."

"Oh." Even in the dim light, he could see her smile.

"Bullet wound?" he repeated, her words registering. "Cecilia told you?"

Lanora shook her head. "No, but I believe I've finally figured you out, William Greydrake."

"What gave me away?"

"Aside from the bullet hole? Which, you should know, Dodger mentioned to Mrs. Smith as belonging to Lord Lefthook."

"That's my fault. I told him to trust you." Because he did.

"Lethbridge gave me the final clues." Her voice was midnight soft. "There was the way you grew up, but also the writing tools. He placed them on the left side of the desk. That's why the second will wasn't knocked off. It was all to the left, as if that was the hand he knew you would use to sign. Then I recalled your signature below the list, smudged, as if signed with your left hand."

She pulled her hand from his, but only to reach across him for the other. His knuckles were a blur in the moonlight, but he knew they bore evidence of being buried in Lethbridge's face. She ran gentle fingers across them. "And you hit him with this hand."

William shifted, and wondered if she understood the effect of her fingers on his body. He was in no state for antics of any sort, and Cecilia would kill him if he tore his stiches again, assuming he didn't die doing it. Which seemed more and more worth the risk with each stroke of her fingers. He drew in a long breath and forced calm.

Lanora raised wide eyes to his. "Are you in pain?" Her hand went to his forehead again. "Shall I wake Lady Cecilia?"

He chuckled. She had no notion of the effect she had. He would educate her, once they were properly wed. "I'm well enough. There's no need for Cecilia."

"You're sure?" Lanora dropped her gaze. She pressed her lips together, as she did when she wasn't sure if she wished to voice her thoughts.

He brushed his fingers across her cheek. "What is it?"

She shrugged, her gaze on the coverlet. "You and Lady Cecilia seem very close and she is, well, rather perfect. And terribly kind. It's difficult for me to believe…that is, if you say it's all in the past, I'll believe you. I should never hold your past against you, William. Not that there's anything wrong in it," she added.

"Lanora, there's nothing between Cecilia and I save friendship, and never has been." Gently, he placed a finger beneath her chin and tipped up her face so that she was forced to look at him. "She is all the things you describe, but she was never for me. I've been in love with another since I was a boy, and she was but a girl. I've been reading Darington's stories of his daughter, somewhere in the countryside in England, for half my life. I was too entranced by her to ever look at Cecilia that way. I love Darington's daughter and I always will."

"Oh. I see." She jerked her chin away and started to stand.

William caught her hand. Fool that he was, he'd left out a rather important piece of information. "I mean you, Lanora. You're Darington's daughter. I've loved you for years."

She stared down at him, face crumpled with hurt. She pulled free. Tears glittered in the moonlight. "You are fevered. I should fetch Lady Cecilia."

He started to sit up. He'd made a muddle of things. "No, you don't understand. There is no Darington."

Lanora was at his side. She pressed him back down to the bed. "You'll hurt yourself. Don't get up. I'll return, but let me fetch her. You worry me."

He captured her hand firmly in one of his, for fear she would go, and used his other to smooth tears from her cheeks. "You don't need to fetch Cecilia, or to cry over me. I'm a fool. Let me begin again."

Lanora offered a smile that trembled at the edges.

"There is no Mr. Darington. There never was. Your father invented him."

"You're unwell. It's the bullet wound."

"That's why they have the same handwriting. They are the same man. When your mother died, your grandfather wouldn't fund your father's expedition to Egypt. The marquess did, in exchange for a story that would explain where I'd been for ten years."

"My father invented Mr. Darington?"

William nodded.

"And he's been writing to you about me for years?"

"Yes."

"You swear that's the truth?" She sounded stunned.

"I swear on my honor, my heart, anything and everything. It's the truth."

She looked away from him, stared at nothing, her eyes bright in the moonlight. "I was never sure if he read my letters."

"He must have."

"But, all the things Mr. Darington has done. The adventures. The exploits."

"Your father."

"I can hardly believe it." She sounded as if she did not.

"I had it from the marquess's mouth moments before he died."

"Would he have lied? To trick you?"

"Not this time. He was overjoyed to impart the news. He thought it would turn me against your father."

She turned back to him, worried. "Did it?"

"No." William understood. He sympathized with Duke Solworth's need to run from his pain, and wouldn't let a single, simple lie tarnish their friendship.

"I'm sorry your father died," Lanora said, her voice soft.

"I'm not." William didn't hide the bitterness in his tone.

She considered that. "Lethbridge said he knew about your brother." Her tentative tone made the statement a question.

William closed his eyes for a moment. She had a right to know. He wanted her to. Someone must, aside from the dead marquess and Lethbridge. Even Cecilia didn't know. "When I was four, the marquess beat my older brother, Charles, to death, because he was afraid of horses. Charles was six."

Lanora gasped.

"He'd always been violent, but he'd never gone that far. My mother took me, and she ran. She didn't take much with her, for she made her escape quickly. She had nowhere to go he couldn't find her. A man has all legal right to his wife and child. We disappeared into the streets of London. She worked as a washwoman."

William's mind filled with images of that life. The cold winters. Hunger a daily companion. Learning to defend what was his, little though it was. "It wasn't a bad life. It wasn't a good one, either."

"You were so young," Lanora said. "Your poor mother."

"There was happiness. We had a slate. She taught me to read, to speak Italian and French. My figures. She made stories of history and the classics. Likely, I learned more at her side than I ever would have from some dry tutor."

"How did he find you?"

It was the question, the memory, he dreaded. He swallowed. "When we left the marquess, she didn't tell me why. I didn't know Charles was gone, only that we had to leave. When I was fourteen, she fell ill. I did all I could for extra coin, to buy treatments from that hack of a doctor who keeps shop at the edge of the borough." He took another breath, aware his words were torn with anger, guilt and grief.

"You don't have to tell me." Lanora's voice was gentle, a soothing balm. "I don't need to know your past, only the man you've become."

He squeezed her hand tighter in his. "Every man is his past. I want you to know." He gathered calm to him. "She grew so ill, she became delirious. I knew the tonics weren't helping. I had vague memories of the marquess, the staff. Clean rooms and beds. I went to find him. It didn't take long. He knew me the moment he set eyes on me. He seemed...happy. The happiest I've ever known him to be."

William stared toward the dark ceiling. He could picture it all clearly, even after a dozen years. "I took him to her. Even delirious, she knew him. She screamed. He had her taken away. I went to his home. He said he was having her taken care of. I begged to see her. Finally, I was allowed."

A servant had taken him in a rented hackney, but had been told not to enter. No one was to know who William visited that day at the prison. A jailer who wasn't told his name brought him to his mother, huddled on a cot in a cell. "I wasn't allowed in the cell. She was too ill to come to the bars. That's when she told me why we'd left, what happened to Charles. She told me, too, to do as the marquess asked. Always. She said a man filled with so much hatred couldn't live long, and then I would be free of him, but for now I must not anger him."

He shook his head, trying to scatter the memories. Her tears as she said she loved him. The hard knowledge, as the jailer returned, that he would never see her again.

He cleared his throat. "The marquess never told anyone. The world thought my mother had gone mad, and then died. Madelina doesn't know she was born out of wedlock, and her mother never knew she wasn't legally married to the old man. Not that knowing would have saved her when he pushed her down the stairs."

"Pushed her down the stairs?" Lanora repeated, her voice as dazed as her dimly seen expression.

"There's no proof. He said she fell." Another surge of guilt welled in him. "I knew he beat her. I should have intervened."

"You were a boy."

"I was seventeen when she died." Old enough to act.

"So when he married Cecilia, you hid her?"

William nodded. "I did."

He leaned his head back on the pillow, closed his eyes. All of the memories he kept hidden, all spilled from him in so short a time. God help him, he was tired.

Lanora withdrew her hand. He realized he'd been holding it too tight. Her weight shifted. He kept his eyes shut, not wanting to see her go, even though he hoped she would return. She was Lanora, Darington's daughter. She would forgive all, understand, and love him. That was how it must be. Still, it hurt when she stood to leave.

The bed shifted. Warmth spread along his right side. Lanora took his arm, wrapping it about her shoulders as she snuggled against him. Her head settled on his chest. She put an arm about him, careful to avoid his stitches.

William kept his eyes closed, not wanting vision to ruin this dream. The honeysuckle scent of her enveloped him. He could almost believe they were in the country, far from London, at peace. That peace stole through him, easing muscles tensed by the anguish of the past. His arm about Lanora, William drifted to sleep, knowing this was how he wanted to spend every night, for the rest of his life.

EPILOGUE

William, someone is here to see you." Cecilia burst into his dressing room. William's valet discreetly withdrew.

William, in the act of tying his cravat, glanced at her in the mirror. She looked lovely in her new dress, special for his wedding day. Lanora, who didn't care for shopping, had been very patient in going with Cecilia to arrange for her first new wardrobe in years. They'd also taken his sister, Madelina, who would have her come out soon. Grace, however, was the only one of the four who had any notion of style. He was fortunate she regularly went along. All three women were very kind to William's shy younger sister.

They stayed in his London townhouse. He'd given up Cecilia's house, bringing both her and Madelina to his. He wasn't sure what to do with the ancestral home. None of them cared to live with the memories there.

"Cecilia, you oughtn't barge into a man's room." He untied the cravat and tossed it aside, displeased with the outcome. He reached for a freshly starched one. It must be perfect.

"I certainly can. For one thing, I've stitched you up often enough to have seen just about all of you." She came forward, batting his hands away so she could tie his cravat. "For another, I am your mother."

"And an adorable mother you are, for all you're two years my junior, but the fact remains that a man's quarters are sacrosanct."

"Oh? So, when Lanora moves in this afternoon, she won't be permitted in these rooms?" She tied the cravat with easy precision, then fluffed it.

William's face split into a too-wide grin. He knew he looked like a besotted fool, there was a mirror before him to prove it, but he didn't care. "Lanora will be permitted in any of my rooms she likes, and all the more reason for you to knock."

Cecilia stepped back, looking him up and down. "Never fear, I shall. I may have seen nearly all of you, but I have no inclination to view the last bit."

"You're a scandalous creature, Cecilia Greydrake."

"I'm a widow. I follow the papers. We are made to be scandalous. More importantly, someone is here to see you." Her eyes were bright, joyful even for Cecilia.

"I'm not taking callers. We have to leave soon. Can't whoever it is wait for a day when I'm not marrying?"

"Definitely not. Now, I've put him in the front parlor. Hurry along." She made a shooing gesture.

William permitted himself to be driven from the room. Cecilia lingered behind as he descended the staircase. Obviously, he was meant to meet the gentleman alone. He strode into the parlor.

The man was well-garbed, nearly as tall as William. He appeared near his fortieth year, but no silver flecked jet black hair, unfashionably short. There was an ease to his stance, a power to his build that belied his apparent age. That vigor, that self-assurance…though William had never before met him in person, he knew the caller.

William came forward, offering his hand. "Who do I have the pleasure of addressing today, sir?"

The man's handshake was firm. "Robert Hadler, Duke of Solworth."

"I'm pleased to meet you, my lord."

"You were expecting someone else on the day you're to wed my daughter?"

"I was unsure. I thought I might be addressing Mr. Darington, renown explorer."

Solworth grinned, his teeth white in a tanned face. "Unfortunately, Darington had to remain in Egypt. He never leaves there, poor fellow."

"More's the pity. I should like to thank him most warmly for being my confidant all these years."

Solworth looked William up and down, assessing. "You've grown into a fine man, William. I know it's not my place to say, but I'm proud of you."

William squared his shoulders, startled by how much those words meant to him. "I do my best, my lord."

"And far better than most men. Shame you and Lanora have so much work before you here. Could use a man like you in Egypt."

"I'll keep that in mind, my lord. Thank you."

"Come along. Let the ladies take your carriage. I've brought mine. Let's get you to my daughter."

William followed Solworth out, a bit bemused. It was obvious the duke was accustomed to giving orders. William collected his hat and gloves. He cast a look about the foyer. When next he set foot in his home, of late filled with Cecilia's laughter and Madelina's soft voice, Lanora would be by his side. Then, his life would be perfect as he'd never thought to dream it could be. That happy thought in mind, he followed Lanora's father out.

"When did you arrive?" William asked once they were seated in the carriage.

"Yesterday. I don't mind saying, I was worried for a spell. We had rough seas for the crossing." Solworth's expression grew distant. "It's been a long time since I laid eyes on England, or Lanora. She grew up."

William wasn't sure how to answer that, so he returned the conversation to the duke's journey. The ride to the church wasn't long. At first their conversation was stilted, but soon William and Solworth were conversing as old friends. William felt at ease with this man, the only person aside from Lanora who knew all his secrets. Only one point of contention stood between them, and it wasn't the lie of Darington.

The carriage drew to a halt. "Ready?" Solworth asked.

"I have one question, my lord."

Solworth raised his brows.

"Lanora wrote to you often, yet she rarely heard from you. She believed you didn't read her letters, yet I know you did. You reported her every deed to me. Why not write your daughter? She missed you. She wanted to know her father."

Solworth was silent. William began to feel he'd spoken out of turn. Certainly, it wasn't a question for his wedding day.

"Because I wasn't coming home, and I wasn't bringing her to Egypt," he finally said. "Each time I wrote, I only disappointed her." Solworth shrugged. "You don't know the pain of breaking your child's heart."

William did not, nor could he imagine the pain of breaking Lanora's. It was one heartache he would never have to know, for he would never give her cause for anguish. "You're right, I don't know, nor quite understand."

"It would have killed me to come home, but Egypt was no place for her. Someday, when you have a child, you'll see that."

William nodded. He wasn't convinced, but sensed that was all the explanation he would have.

Solworth leaned forward. "Never hurt her, William."

"I won't, my lord." It was a promise he could make with all sincerity.

Solworth smiled. "I know. Now, shall we? You don't want to be late."

They left the carriage and strode up the steps. Entering the church, William heard his name whispered. He turned toward the sound. "Lanora?"

"I have to speak to you," she whispered, hidden behind a screen in the vestibule.

William looked to Solworth, who shrugged. William strode over to the screen.

"You've met my father?" Lanora asked, her voice low.

"I have."

"You like him?"

"Of course." Was that her concern?

"Good. Could you send him into the chapel? I would like to speak with you in private."

"Isn't it ill luck?"

"William, that's ridiculous. You can close your eyes if you like, but you and I are speaking."

William shook his head. He crossed back to Solworth. "Don't linger on my account, my lord. Lanora wishes a quick word."

"Don't be long," Solworth said. He nodded to William, then toward the screen, and entered the chapel.

William returned to Lanora, skirting the screen. Taking his hand, she pulled him through a doorway and into a small room. Relinquishing her grip, she turned to face him.

Her gown was simple, for her beauty required no adornment. Her silken black hair was arranged to curl about her face, longer locks draped over her shoulder. Gems sparkled against the midnight hue, but none were as bright as her emerald eyes. She was nothing short of perfection.

"You wish to speak?" William clasped his hands behind his back to avoid reaching for her.

"There's something I must tell you before we marry."

He frowned. "You have a secret?"

"No, I doubt that. Only something I must say."

His frown deepened. "Well?"

She took a step closer. Her hands came to rest on his coat front. He cursed the layers of fabric that muted her touch. "It's only that, before we wed, I wanted to be sure to tell you…" She studied his face. "I love you, William Greydrake."

A grin transformed his features.

"You have nothing to say to that?" she asked, surprised.

"What shall I say?"

"You could say it back, or seem relieved. You've told me you love me, more than once." She looked bewildered. "If it were me, I'd be in fits. I'd be worried sick, not having heard those words from you. I mean, I've felt it for some time now, maybe even since my aunt introduced us, but every time you said it, I was always too surprised to hear it to say it back, and... Will you stop grinning?"

"Only if you stop rambling on in so adorable a manner."

"You haven't been the least bit worried I haven't told you I love you?"

William shook his head. "Not the slightest."

Lanora narrowed her eyes. "Why not?"

"Because I've always known you do."

Her eyes flashed a bright green, nearly mesmerizing. "You were so sure, you didn't need to hear me say it? So certain of your charm?"

"I was. I am."

"You're an insufferable rake."

He couldn't resist. He slid his arm around her, pulling her against him. "Yes, but I'm your insufferable rake." He lowered his mouth to hers and kissed her.

It wouldn't have stopped there, not this time, but someone cleared her throat.

"William," Cecilia snapped.

Reluctantly, he lifted his head. A glance showed Cecilia, Grace and Lady Edith arrayed just inside the little room. It was a wonder they'd entered unnoticed, but he'd been quite distracted.

"William, I'm escorting you to the front of the church." Cecilia's tone was firm, but her eyes danced.

"And you are coming with us while we straighten your dress, young woman," Lady Edith said.

Something barked. William blinked, realizing the Skye Terrier peeked out from behind Lady Edith's billowing skirt.

"Shush," she scolded the dog, her expression softening.

"Come along, Lanora," Grace said. "I daresay there will be plenty of time for that later, once you're properly wed."

William looked down at Lanora, still in his arms. "Thank you."

"For marrying you?"

"For loving me."

"I do love you," she said. "More than anything."

"I love you too." He kissed her again, finding her more than willing, deaf to the protests.

LOOK FOR THE DUKE'S WIDOW, BOOK TWO IN THE UNDER THE
SHADOW OF THE MARQUESS SERIES SUMMER 2018

FOR NOW, ENOY A SPECIAL EXCERPT FROM
The Marriage Maker Series

One Good Gentleman

The Marriage Maker Book Five
Rules of Refinement

Summer Hanford

RULES OF REFINEMENT

Noblemen aren't always honorable... but a rake is always charming

In a narrow lane off Edinburgh's illustrious Charlotte Square, stands a town house that is not quite as impressive as nearby residences, but remains a place of distinction. An air of quiet dignity is maintained by the courtyard that fronts the street, while privacy is assured by a wrought-iron gateway. This house is Lady Peddington's School for Young Ladies and is owned and run by Lady Honoria Peddington.

Girls fortunate enough to attend the academy are instructed in all aspects of proper comportment with emphasis on the importance of a pleasing demeanor and appearance, grace and good manners, the skills a lady needs to run a large, well-to-do household, and – of course - the necessity and advantages of an impeccable reputation. Scandal, the girls are warned, must be avoided at all costs.

Lady Peddington's own reputation is the finest, and all Edinburgh considers her above reproach. She is especially well-loved by the affluent merchants and lesser gentry who live on the fringes of the city's New Town where she operates her school. These clients appreciate her knack at finding affluent husbands for their daughters. No one suspects that her knowledge of men comes from the long-ago days when she wasn't Lady Honoria Peddington, but simply Honey Pedding who ran a well-doing Glasgow brothel.

Those skills, though secret, still serve her well, for when her school's famed graduation balls fail to secure suitable husbands for some of her more high-spirited girls, other gentlemen come to the fore, eager to accept these gems as pampered mistresses. So, however a girl's heart might lean, Lady Peddington's School for Young Ladies guarantees happiness for all.

Her virtue or her dreams…which must she abandon?

Emilia Glasbarr doesn't want to be a country miss with a yard full of geese and a scant handful of neighbors. She wants the music, theatre and art found in Scotland's capital city. She's sunk her every resource into finishing school to find a city-dwelling husband. Unfortunately, the only man interested wants her for a far less savory purpose.

CHAPTER ONE

AT THE END OF EACH SEASON, Lady Peddington's School for Young Ladies threw not one, or even two, but four balls over the course of four weeks. If a young woman couldn't meet the man of her dreams in that length of time, well, she'd best hope a man awaited her at home because four was the schools' more than generous limit. To Miss Emilia Glasbarr's dismay, the first of these balls was stuttering to an end, and she still lacked a suitor.

Emilia huddled near the refreshments table and tried to untangle the scene before her. Many of the girls, certainly the ones already spoken for, had retired for the evening. Those who remained, behaved with a lack of propriety that Emilia found moderately shocking. Gloves were removed. Laughter, not polite titters, sounded. Footmen had appeared to snuff out most of the candles, leaving the vast ballroom enshrouded in flickering half-light. Most disconcerting, the few instructors who still chaperone turned a blind eye. Only Emilia's desperation not to live out the remainder of her days as a country Miss kept her there. Normally, she would retreat from such a scene.

A waltz began and Emilia stifled a gasp. No respectable young woman danced the waltz. They'd been taught as much at the very school in which she stood. Gentlemen reached out, clasped ladies close. Distressed by the bedlam before her, Emilia turned away from the whirling figures. She swallowed, her throat dry, and reached for a glass of punch.

The gulp she took burned the whole way down, laced with some strong spirit. She raised incredulous eyes to the woman who oversaw the punch table, their etiquette instructor, and received a wink. Disconcerted, Emilia set out around the edge of the room, unsure what to do with the glass she held. Putting the punch down now would be ill-mannered, but she dared not drink more. The one gulp already left her dizzy.

A gentleman strode toward her. Emilia dropped her gaze demurely. She knew who he was, for the school kept miniatures of all the local nobility, and she knew he wasn't there to find a wife. He was already wed. She could only assume he came to support the school, to help Lady Peddington's students practice the art of dancing at a real social engagement, not under the eyes of an instructor.

She suppressed a sigh of disappointment that an eligible gentleman refused to appear, for well-bred ladies didn't sigh, and angled toward the wall to give him room to pass without interfering with the dancers. She stopped in surprise when he stepped in front of her. His too-strong cologne assailed her nostrils. Punch sloshed onto her gloved fingers. Her face heated at her clumsiness.

His eyes dipped toward the glass for a moment. "Partaking of Lady Peddington's famous midnight punch, I see." His accent was urbane. Dark eyes looked down at her from under oiled brown hair.

"Midnight punch?" she repeated, confused.

"No need to play coy. I love Lady Peddington's special midnight brew, and a girl who drinks it." He leaned forward as he spoke and used his six inches of superior height to look down the front of her white muslin gown.

Emilia's blush deepened. "I've only taken one sip." She almost choked on her own inanity, but what was one to say to that statement, or that look? He wasn't behaving the way they'd been taught men should behave, let alone married members of the peerage.

"You should drink up then, dear girl." He wrapped a hand around hers and lifted the glass to her lips.

Emilia was too shocked by his hand on hers to protest. She gagged as the heavily laced punch tumbled into her mouth. She choked it down, for one could hardly spit up on a viscount.

"That's better," he said when the glass was empty. He dabbed at the corners of her mouth with a glove-encased thumb.

Emilia watched him through eyes as wide as saucers. "My lord," she managed to gasp out.

His smile was pleased. "So, you know who I am?"

"Indeed, I do, Lord Ailbeart, but I'm sure we've never met, and certainly do no' know each other well enough for you to put your hands on me."

He raised thick eyebrows. "Don't we? Perhaps you would care for a bit more punch?"

"I most certainly would not." Already the room had begun a gentle spin. Emilia rarely tasted wine, and had eaten lightly, nervous for the dance. Whatever was in the punch, and she suspected scotch, had gone straight to her head.

Far from appearing offended by her rejoinder, the viscount grinned. His fingers grazed her cheek as he tugged on one of her yellow curls before letting it spring back into place. "Spirited, aren't you? I want a spirited mistress this time. The last one was too well trained. A lady can be too polished."

Emilia was doubly upset she'd consumed the punch, for she had nothing to throw in his face. "Did I hear you suggest I be your mistress, my lord?" she gritted out. She hadn't spent her entire dowry on finishing school to become this man's plaything.

"I knew I'd picked a good one in you." His grin was smug.

Emilia glared through narrowed hazel eyes. "Picked?"

"Aye. I told the other fellows, stay clear of that golden-haired beauty. She's mine." He spoke in a warm, almost sweet tone, as if praising a favored pet. His gaze roamed over her.

Emilia drew in a harsh breath, too offended to be embarrassed. "I do not believe that is for you to say, my lord."

"But it is, and since I have, no one else will dare dance with you." He closed the distance between them, his voice low and suddenly edged with malice. "And when you find yourself all alone at the end of the fourth ball, with the choice of a fine house in the heart of Edinburgh or slogging back to whatever obscure corner of the countryside you crawled in from, you'll realize that being my most prized possession is more desirable."

He grabbed the back of her neck, yanked her forward and kissed her. It was a brief, rough kiss that left her reeling as he sauntered away. Emilia was aghast. She jerked her gaze around the room, but no one seemed to have noticed. Mortified, breath ragged, she fled the ballroom.

Emilia clutched her skirt in both hands to keep the hem off the floor and ran through the dim halls of Lady Peddington's School. The stench of Viscount Dunreid's cologne clung to her. She didn't know where she went until she burst through the door to the drawing classroom, the room where she always felt happiest. To her relief, Missus Millview, the drawing instructor, was there.

"Miss Glasbarr?" Missus Millview rose from her chair. "Whatever is the matter? What are you doing here? It's well after midnight."

She stumbled across the room toward her instructor. "Lord Ailbeart, that is, Viscount Dunreid kissed me," she blurted. "I didnae want him to, but he did." She burst into tears.

Missus Millview reached her side and wrapped Emilia in a warm embrace. "There, there, my dear child," she murmured. "You shouldn't be up after midnight. You aren't the sort. There's been an error."

Emilia sniffed. "An error?" Did midnight signify in some way? "I don't understand."

Missus Millview shook her head, eyes sympathetic in her long face. "It's nothing, child, nothing at all. Only that you should retire earlier at the next ball, to avoid this sort of thing. Gentlemen tend to get out of hand in the later hours."

"They do?" Emilia pulled away. She wiped at her cheeks with the heels of her hands.

"Of course." Missus Millview gave her a gentle smile. "You dance the early dances from now on and retire before midnight, and forget this incident with Lord Ailbeart ever occurred."

"But I can't," Emilia cried. "No one will dance with me. Not one gentleman asked. Lord Ailbeart said he warned them away because I'm to be...to be..." She couldn't say it aloud, what he'd propositioned. "What am I to do? I convinced my parents to let me use the money they set aside for my dowry to come here. I told them a man would prefer a cultured bride over one with a small sum. I don't want to go back to the country. I want to stay here where there is music and art."

Missus Millview's brow creased, her look one of compassion. Emilia glanced around the nearly dark room. Why was Missus Ailbeart in her classroom at that hour? She took in the desk. The scattered candle stubs illuminated receipts and pages filled with rows of numbers.

Missus Millview followed her gaze. She let out a sigh, and passed a hand over tired eyes. "Yes, we must all worry about our funds, child."

Concern of another sort stole through Emilia. Missus Millview was a good person, and her favorite instructor. "Is there anything I can do?"

"Do?" Missus Millview shook her head. "No. I'll be well enough, so long as I keep my place here." She pressed her lips into a tight frown and dragged her gaze from her desk, back to Emilia. "I should like to help you, child. You aren't one who should have been brought to Lord Ailbeart's attention. I suspect it's your beauty that's the trouble, not that you can help that."

Emilia blinked. Beauty? She knew she had no obvious flaws in appearance, but she hardly thought she had sufficient beauty to garner attention, especially from a viscount. "You can help me?" Her voice caught at the hope that surged within her.

Missus Millview looked to her pages of numbers again. She gave a sharp nod. "I can, but you must promise not to tell any of the other girls. I can't lose my place here. I'm not young or beautiful enough to make my way if I do."

"I promise," Emilia said eagerly. "Please, what can I do? I simply want to marry a kind man. I do no' need a title, or wealth, or much of anything, really. Just a gentleman who lives in the city."

"You won't tell those three friends of yours?" Missus Millview eyed her shrewdly. "I know how inseparable you four are, and I suspect they may be in the same boat. You must promise not to tell them what I'll reveal to you, child. I've come to care for you, but a woman alone in this world must look out for herself."

Emilia bit back a hasty acceptance. Her friends had all retired earlier as, apparently, proper young women did. They'd been discouraged as they'd also lacked admirers. Could she consign any of them to men like Lord Ailbeart?

She drew in a breath. She couldn't, but she would find a way to help without breaking Missus Millview's confidence. "I promise I won't tell the other girls, even my friends."

Missus Millview offered a relieved smile. "Well then, this should help you." She crossed to the desk, then pulled free a clean page and began to write.

Emilia followed her. She looked over Missus Millview's shoulder to take in the elegantly penned address and a name. "Sir Stirling James," she read aloud.

Missus Millview turned to offer the page. "Yes. They call him The Marriage Maker. If anyone can help you, he can." Her face went stern, as it did when Emilia attempted anything less than her best work. "But don't forget your promise."

"I won't, Missus Millview." Emilia folded the page in half. "Thank you."

"You're a good child," Missus Millview said. "Too good for the likes of Viscount Dunreid. Can you reach your chamber well enough?"

Emilia thought about the empty halls. No one had stopped her on her way to the classroom. She nodded. "I can." She gave Missus Millview a quick hug. "Thank you. You've saved me, and I won't tell the others."

Missus Millview sighed and shook her head. "I hope not, child, I truly do."

Emilia left with a lighter heart than she'd had in hours. She took the back way to her room, thankful the halls and stairs were as blissfully empty as she'd hoped. As she walked, she formulated a plan. She would write this Sir Stirling James now, before bed. She would tell him of her plight, and include a small portrait she'd done of herself, on the chance she really was as pretty as Missus Millview said.

In fact, she would include portraits of her three friends as well, and beg him to help them all. Missus Millview had made her swear not to tell any of the other girls about Sir Stirling James. That didn't mean Emilia couldn't tell him about them. She smiled as she reached the safety of her room and lit a candle, pleased with her plan.

CHAPTER TWO

ROBERT BANBROOK SAT ALONE AT a table in his club, staring into a half-empty glass of scotch. The only good thing about Scotland, as far as he was concerned. One up, then, on England. The Irish had Irish Whiskey, the Scots had Scottish Whisky. What did England offer a man to drown his sorrows? Gin. Robert shuddered at the thought. He swallowed the rest of the glass to dispel the memory of the revolting stuff.

"You look a bit peaked there, Banbrook," a jovial voice said. A large hand clasped his shoulder briefly.

Robert looked up from his empty tumbler and squinted to bring Sir Stirling James into focus. Stirling pulled out a chair and seated himself at the table.

"I'm as fine as a fiddle, Stirling, I can assure you." Robert reached for the nearly empty decanter before him. He missed once, but claimed it on the second try. He flashed Stirling a grin, proud of his success. "You see? Fine as a fiddle," Robert repeated.

Liquid sloshed onto his fingers and he looked down. Whisky tumbled from the mouth of the crystal decanter and over the hand clasping the tumbler. Furrowing his brow in concentration, he angled the bottle to get more into the glass.

"I'm glad to hear it, Banbrook, because I was worried you'd spent the past three days in this club drinking yourself to death." Stirling lifted an arm and waved. A footman hurried over with a cloth to sop up the spilled liquor.

"Oh, I have. I am." Robert offered a grin, though he could hardly feel his face.

"I take it this ill-conceived effort has to do with a certain young lady?" Stirling asked as the footman mopped the spill.

"You, Geoffrey, bring me another bottle," Robert said to the footman. He turned back to Stirling. "You use the word *lady* loosely."

"I find that doubtful." Stirling nodded toward the footman. "John will ignore your request." Stirling emphasized the man's name. "The entire staff will. I've had you cut off."

Robert let out a mumbled curse. The footman departed without looking at him. A glance showed no others near.

"Can't you leave me to drink myself to death in peace?" Robert asked. He squinted at the older gentleman. "You used to be fun." He knocked back his drink and realized very little whisky had made its way into his glass.

"Oh, I have something fun planned, never fear." Stirling stood and gestured again.

Footsteps sounded behind Robert. He craned his neck in an effort to see who approached. Two of the burlier footmen, their faces set, marched toward him. Or was there one and he was seeing the man twice? He blinked several times, but neither of the two disappeared.

Large hands clasped his arms and lifted him from the chair. At least four hands, so at least two of the fellows, then. Or was that three? The empty tumbler slipped free of his grasp to hit the table with a thunk.

The sound drew his attention as the men got him to his feet. Sad empty tumbler. All it wanted was to do its duty by him. So loyal. Not like women.

Stirling appeared at his side, swaying like a storm-tossed schooner. "What do you think, Banbrook, can you walk?"

Robert shook off the hands and straightened. "I most certainly can. What do you take me for?" He raised his chin, endeavoring to stare Stirling down, but his chin wouldn't stop. It went up and up. Robert's head tilted back. He'd never taken time to properly contemplate the ceiling of his club before. One always overlooked the details.

Four hands gripped him and stood him upright again when he started to topple backward. Stirling, still swaying, appeared greatly amused. He gestured and the hands began to half walk, half carry Robert.

The faces of other gentlemen at the club moved in a slow spiral around him as they crossed the room. Most were turned his way. Expressions ranged from sympathetic to disgusted. Robert would have taken careful note of who owned the latter, but the names of his peers were strangely absent from his brain. Maybe they were all named Geoffrey. The idea inclined him to laugh, but he didn't want to amuse Stirling any further.

The hands didn't toss him from the club as he half-expected, but instead took him up the steps and into one of the private rooms, furnished with a bed, desk, chairs and table. Inside stood a large, full washtub, as well. He had just enough sense to wonder why no steam rose from the tub before he was picked up and plunked, fully clothed, into the chilly water.

In shock, he slid under the surface. He came up gasping for air. Rapid blinking brought Stirling into view beside the tub. Robert unleashed a stream of invectives. Stirling gestured. A large hand settled on Robert's head and pushed him back under, then let him up immediately.

"Feeling better yet?" Stirling asked as Robert's head cleared the surface once more.

"You bloody, rat-faced, son-of-a—" A gesture from Stirling. Robert went down into the water again. He flailed at the hand, but it didn't remain on his head long enough to strike. He pushed himself to the surface, spitting water. "Do you mean to kill me?"

Stirling looked down at him, arms crossed, expression contemplative. "I thought death was your goal."

"You bloody well know it's not, you madman. This water is damned cold."

"Here in Scotland, we call it refreshing."

"Well I'm a bloody Englishman and I don't appreciate being dunked in a trough." Robert pushed a hand over his face, skimming away water. "What are you playing at, Stirling?"

"Playing?" Stirling shook his head. "No. I've a favor to ask, actually."

"A favor?" Robert gaped. He stood. Water streamed from his hair, coat, flattened cravat, everywhere. "This is you asking for a favor?"

"I need you clear-headed enough to comprehend my words." Stirling's tone was reasonable, but amusement lurked in his features.

Robert muttered a few choice curses as he stepped over the edge of the tub. Water sloshed across the floor. One of the footmen immediately began to wipe it up. The other offered Robert a towel, his expression neutral.

Robert took the proffered cloth and mopped at his face. "Look what you've done to my jacket. My vest." He let out another curse. "My boots, man. Look what you've done to my boots."

"Put them by the fire. John will take your clothes and see them made right."

Robert turned to take in the cheery blaze. Now that his vision was clearer, he also noticed a set of clothes laid out, as well as a nightshirt and robe. His clothes. His nightshirt and robe.

He cast Stirling an incredulous look. "You've been to my residence?"

"Yes. Your staff are rather worried about you. They haven't seen you in three days."

Robert shook his head, bemused. He crossed to the fire, then began stripping his lean frame. Stirling ordered the tub removed and the floor mopped. Robert shucked his sodden attire.

After toweling dry, he took up his robe. His original intention had been to dress, but weariness had settled. What was the point in dressing, after all? Once he heard Stirling out and sent him on his way, Robert could return to drinking just as easily in a private room in his robe as he could in the public room, dressed.

He belted his robe closed, plopped into an armchair and propped his feet on the nearby stool. He watched with little interest as servants gathered his wet garments, sopped up the last of the water and disappeared. The chair was near the fire, the warmth lulling. His eyes closed.

"Now, about that favor."

Robert forced his lids open to find Stirling seated on the other side of the fireplace. "The answer is no," Robert muttered.

"All I require is for you to attend three balls."

"Balls? With dancing?" Robert scowled. "With ladies?"

"That is generally the way of balls." Stirling rested his elbows on the arms of the chair and steepled his fingers before him.

"Can't. I've sworn off women. For good. No more." Robert shook his head, then regretted the movement as the room bounced. "I will not be jilted a third time, and certainly not again in Scotland. I'm leaving."

"Oh?" Stirling raised an eyebrow. "Headed back to London, are you?"

Robert looked away from those perceptive eyes. He could never go back to London. Every inch of the city reminded him of Cinthia. "Maybe the Continent. Perhaps even France."

"France? Do you intend to get yourself shot?"

Robert shrugged. "At least in France, when a man is jilted, he can drown his sorrow in cognac."

Stirling watched him over his steepled fingers.

Robert resisted an urge to squirm under that gaze. "Or I could hang about Edinburgh for a time. I've nothing against Scotland, just women."

With a sigh, Stirling brought his hands to the chair arms. "Miss Thomas did the right thing, breaking it off with you."

Robert went rigid. "What did you say?"

"Kitty Thomas did the right thing when she broke your engagement."

Anger coiled inside Robert.

"Anyone can see you're still in love with Cinthia."

Robert's anger disappeared like summer rain. Cinthia. The real reason he'd come to Scotland. For two years, they'd been engaged. In London, they were the toast of the *Ton*. Every dance, the theater, the park. Always together. Blissfully happy as they waited for her father to return from his government appointment in India so they could wed.

Then Lord Ailbeart had come along, with Scottish title. He enticed her with his lineage. Whispering that she was meant to be a member of the peerage, Lady Cinthia, Viscountess Dunreid. Not simply Missus Banbrook.

Fool that he was, Robert hadn't been worried. He'd believed in her. Believed in their love. Not until the morning he'd called round and learned she'd left for Scotland did he have any idea Viscount Dunreid had succeeded in his conquest.

He passed a hand over his eyes, weary. "What are you after, Stirling? I've heard rumors of your new game, matchmaking." He eyed the other man. "I'm not looking for another woman to propose to. Twice was enough."

Stirling leaned back in his chair, his expression too innocent to be so. "The last thing I want to do is get some poor girl's hopes up with an introduction to you. Until you get over Viscountess Dunreid, you aren't fit for any woman." He shook his head. "No, I simply need you to help a certain young Miss stave off an aggressive gentleman long enough to find herself a good husband."

Robert frowned. "Stave off? She doesn't want to marry this gentleman? At least she's smart enough to realize as much."

"Aye, she seems an intelligent sort, but I believe the key issue is the offer of the gentleman in question. He wants her, but he has no intention of making her his wife."

So, a cad up to no good and apt to tarnish a young lady's reputation. "I see. She's in need of protection, then, not one of your quick weddings." He scrutinized Stirling. "Why don't you do help the girl?"

"I could, I suppose, but I wouldn't want to deprive you of the honor, or the amusement. Anyone can see you're in need of a bit of distraction."

Robert supposed there was some truth in that. Still, "Escorting some young Miss to dances doesn't sound particularly amusing." It sounded painful.

A sly grin formed on Stirling's face. "Oh, I daresay escorting this young Miss is just what you need. That, and a bit of revenge." He leaned forward in his chair. "You see, Banbrook, Dunreid wants the young lady for his mistress. You, my friend, are going to save her."

www.scarsdalepublishing.com

ABOUT THE AUTHOR

Beginning in 2014, Summer Hanford was offered the privilege of partnering with fan fiction author Renata McMann on her well-loved *Pride and Prejudice* variations. To date, they have over twenty popular *Pride & Prejudice Fan Fiction* stories available, four of which are Amazon Best Sellers. In addition to her work with McMann, Summer is branching out into writing Regency works of her own, with a novel and several short story series upcoming from Scarsdale Publishing.

Born on a dairy farm in Upstate New York, Summer attended university for psychology and art, then went on to do two years each of graduate and doctoral work in Behavioral Neurology. She now lives and writes in Michigan, with her wonderful husband and three obligatory, deliberately spoiled, cats.